Sensational Sports Teams

KINGS OF THE COURT
THE CLEVELAND CAVALIERS

David Aretha

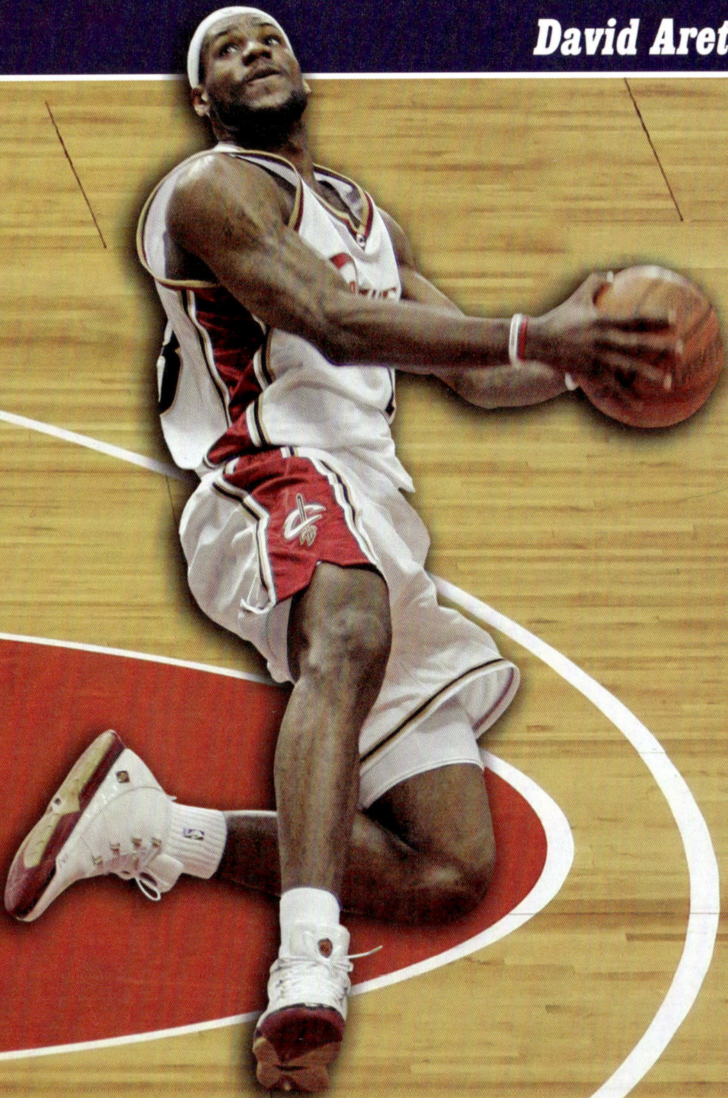

MyReportLinks.com Books
an imprint of

Enslow Publishers, Inc.
Box 398, 40 Industrial Road
Berkeley Heights, NJ 07922
USA

MyReportLinks.com Books, an imprint of Enslow Publishers, Inc. MyReportLinks® is a registered trademark of Enslow Publishers, Inc.

Copyright © 2008 by Enslow Publishers, Inc.

All rights reserved.

No part of this book may be reproduced by any means without the written permission of the publisher.

Library of Congress Cataloging-in-Publication Data

Aretha, David.
   Kings of the court—the Cleveland Cavaliers / David Aretha.
     p. cm. — (Sensational sports teams)
   Includes bibliographical references and index.
   ISBN-13: 978-1-59845-048-4
   ISBN-10: 1-59845-048-4
   1. Cleveland Cavaliers (Basketball team)—Juvenile literature. I. Title.
   GV885.52.C57A74 2004
   796.323'640977132—dc22

2006024153

Printed in the United States of America

10 9 8 7 6 5 4 3 2 1

To Our Readers:
Through the purchase of this book, you and your library gain access to the Report Links that specifically back up this book.
The Publisher will provide access to the Report Links that back up this book and will keep these Report Links up to date on **www.myreportlinks.com** for five years from the book's first publication date.
We have done our best to make sure all Internet addresses in this book were active and appropriate when we went to press. However, the author and the Publisher have no control over, and assume no liability for, the material available on those Internet sites or on other Web sites they may link to.
The usage of the MyReportLinks.com Books Web site is subject to the terms and conditions stated on the Usage Policy Statement on **www.myreportlinks.com**.
A password may be required to access the Report Links that back up this book. The password is found on the bottom of page 4 of this book.
Any comments or suggestions can be sent by e-mail to comments@myreportlinks.com or to the address on the back cover.

Photo Credits: *Akron Beacon Journal,* p. 93; AP/Wide World Photos, pp. 1, 3, 6, 12, 14, 17, 22, 32, 35, 37, 48, 50, 56–57, 60–61, 63, 68, 72–73, 77, 84, 94, 103, 106, 108, 110–111; Basketball-Reference.com, pp. 31, 97; Bill Nochols' *Lakewood Luminary* Page, p. 71; Cleveland Live, Inc., p. 53; ClevelandSeniors.com, pp. 18, 42; CTVglobemedia, p. 109; Dcass and Crunch, pp. 28, 44; ESPN Internet Ventures, p. 64; Maniacal James, LLC, p. 11; Most Valuable Network, LLC, p. 62; Munsey & Suppes, pp. 20, 87; MyReportLinks.com Books, p. 4; Naismith Memorial Basketball Hall of Fame, pp. 75, 99; NBA Media Ventures, LLC, pp. 26, 38, 46, 89, 91, 101; Shutterstock.com, pp. 1, (background), 5; Sports Phenoms, Inc., p. 9; Sun Newspapers, p. 79; Tank Productions, p. 40; The Trust for Public Land, p. 24; The Washington Post Company, pp. 58, 81; USA Basketball, Inc., p. 8.

Cover Photo: AP/Wide World Photos; Shutterstock.com (background).

Cover Description: LeBron James goes up for a reverse dunk.

CONTENTS

	About MyReportLinks.com Books	4
	Cavaliers Time Line	5
1	Home, James	7
2	Fitch's Franchise	15
3	Title Contender	33
4	The King James Era	51
5	Cavs in Charge	69
6	Game Day	85
7	The Heroes	95
	Report Links.............................	114
	Career Stats	116
	Glossary...................................	118
	Chapter Notes..........................	120
	Further Reading.......................	125
	Index......................................	126

About MyReportLinks.com Books

MyReportLinks.com Books
Great Books, Great Links, Great for Research!

The Internet sites featured in this book can save you hours of research time. These Internet sites—we call them **"Report Links"**—are constantly changing, but we keep them up to date on our Web site.

When you see this "Approved Web Site" logo, you will know that we are directing you to a great Internet site that will help you with your research.

Give it a try! Type http://www.myreportlinks.com into your browser, click on the series title and enter the password, then click on the book title, and scroll down to the Report Links listed for this book.

The Report Links will bring you to great source documents, photographs, and illustrations. MyReportLinks.com Books save you time, feature Report Links that are kept up to date, and make report writing easier than ever! A complete listing of the Report Links can be found on pages 114–115 at the back of the book.

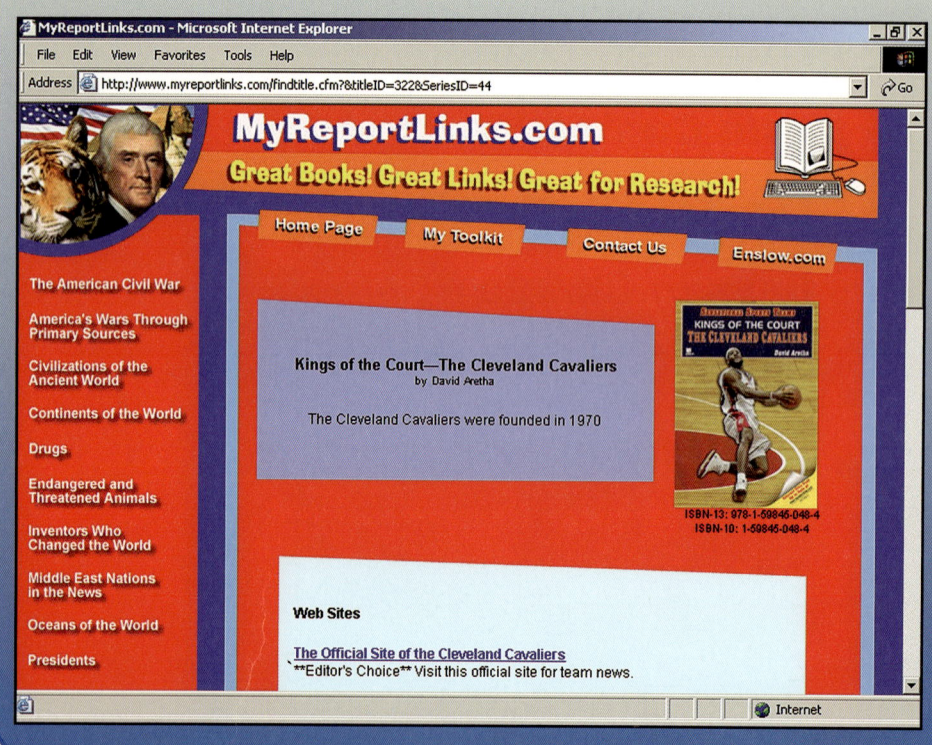

Please see "To Our Readers" on the copyright page for important information about this book, the MyReportLinks.com Web site, and the Report Links that back up this book.

Please enter **CCB1275** if asked for a password.

CAVALIERS TIME LINE

1970-71—Inaugural season. Cavs earn their first win on November 12, 1970, against Portland.

1971-72—Cavs choose Austin Carr with the top pick in the 1971 NBA Draft.

1973-74—Wilkens leads the league in assists per game.

1974-75—Richfield Coliseum becomes the Cavs new home court.

1975-76—Cleveland makes the playoffs for the first time. The Cavs defeat the Washington Bullets in Round 1, before losing to the Boston Celtics in Round 2.

1977-78—The team enjoys its third straight winning season, but falls to the New York Knicks in the first round of the playoffs.

1981-82—The Cavs finish a dismal 15-67, while playing twenty-three different guys.

1983-84—Gordon and George Gund buy the Cleveland Cavaliers.

1984-85—Despite having a losing record (36-46), Cleveland makes the playoffs for the first time in six seasons.

1986-87—Wayne Embry becomes the first African-American general manager in NBA history. Former Cavs guard Lenny Wilkens is named head coach.

1988-89—At 57-25, Cleveland ties for the second best record in the league. However, Michael Jordan and the Chicago Bulls prove to be too much for the Cavs to handle in the playoffs.

1989-90—The Cavs fall to the Philadelphia 76ers in the first round of the playoffs.

1991-92—Cavs finish 57-25, and reach the Eastern Conference Finals.

1992-93—The Cavs win 54 games. Brad Daugherty, Larry Nance, and Mark Price make the All-Star team.

1993-94—Mike Fratello is named head coach. Brad Daugherty become's the franchise's all-time leading scorer.

1994-95—Gund Arena opens as the new home for the Cavs.

1995-96—Cleveland finishes 47-35, making the playoffs for the fifth straight season. The Cavs are swept in the first round by New York.

1997-98—Forward Shawn Kemp is named an All-Star starter.

1999-2000—Cavs name their thirtieth anniversary all-time team: center Brad Daugherty, guards Mark Price and Austin Carr, and forwards Larry Nance and Shawn Kemp.

2001-02—Point guard Andre Miller leads the league in assists.

2002-03—A healthy Zydrunas Ilgauskas makes the All-Star Team, but the Cavs end up at 17-65.

2003-04—Jackpot! Cavs win the right to draft high school superstar LeBron James. Cleveland wins 18 more games than the previous season and James is named Rookie of the Year.

2004-05—Cleveland improves to 42-40, the team's first winning season in five years. James becomes the youngest player ever to record a triple-double. Cavs are purchased by a group led by Dan Gilbert, owner of Quicken Loans.

2005-06—Mike Brown takes over as head coach, and the team finishes 50-32, advancing to the second round of the playoffs. James averages 30.8 ppg in the playoffs.

2006-07—Cavs reach NBA Finals, but lose to the Spurs in four straight.

▲ LeBron James is all smiles after Cleveland made him the top overall pick in the 2003 NBA Draft.

HOME, JAMES 1

The word "curse" is thrown about loosely in sports. The Boston Red Sox were said to have "reversed" one in 2004, when they won their first World Series championship since 1918. Consider, though, that Boston fans had celebrated world championships by the Celtics, Bruins, and Patriots multiple times between Red Sox titles. When it comes to a cursed sports town, fans must consider Cleveland, Ohio.

Not since 1948, when their Indians defeated the Boston Braves in the World Series, have baseball fans in the city off Lake Erie had a world championship to celebrate. The six decades since have seen the Indians bumble through some of the most laughable seasons in baseball history. They lost a staggering 105 games in 1991, and some would argue that even that club was not the worst Indians team in history.

MyReportLinks.com Books

The Cleveland Browns football team was an exception. The Browns enjoyed a remarkable run of success from 1946–57, appearing in eleven league championship games in a twelve-year period. Since their last title in 1964, though, they have broke their fan's hearts more often than not.

Finally, there are the Cleveland Cavaliers. Their history dates to 1970, and never once have they made it to the NBA Finals. But on May 22, 2003, the Cavaliers overcame the town's traditional sports jinx with a win in the NBA Draft Lottery. This allowed them to select home-state hero and future superstar LeBron James.

The odds were in their favor on lottery day. Cleveland and Denver had tied for the worst

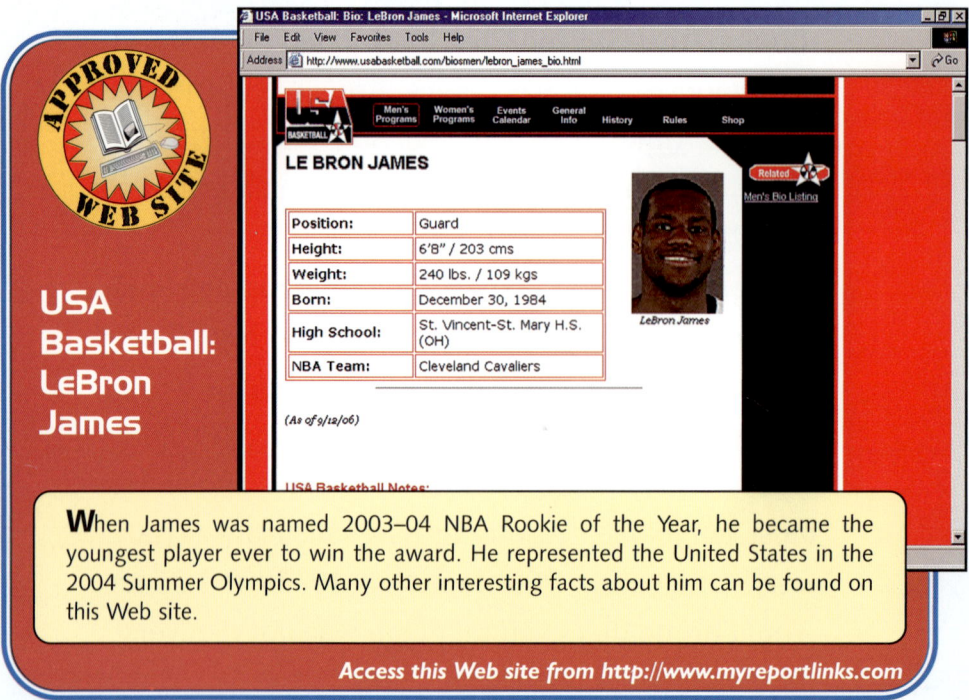

USA Basketball: LeBron James

When James was named 2003–04 NBA Rookie of the Year, he became the youngest player ever to win the award. He represented the United States in the 2004 Summer Olympics. Many other interesting facts about him can be found on this Web site.

Access this Web site from http://www.myreportlinks.com

Home, James

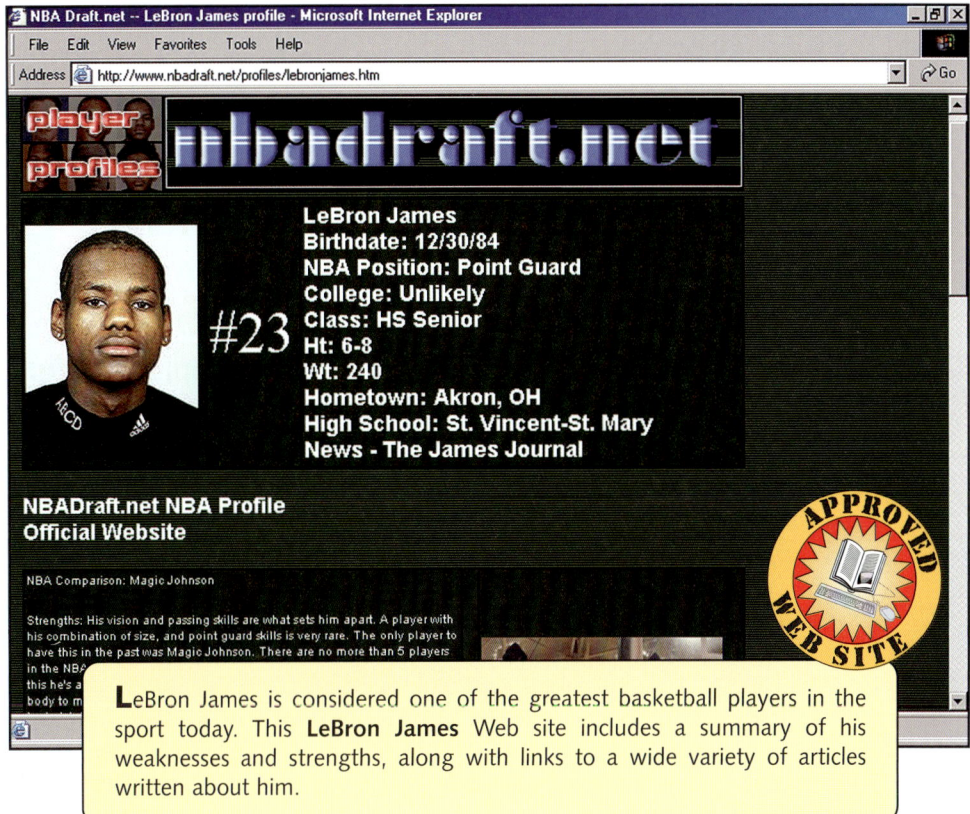

LeBron James is considered one of the greatest basketball players in the sport today. This **LeBron James** Web site includes a summary of his weaknesses and strengths, along with links to a wide variety of articles written about him.

record in the NBA the previous season at 17–65. Each club received 225 Ping-Pong-ball combinations in the weighted system used to determine the top three picks in the upcoming draft. That is, both the Cavaliers and Nuggets had a 22.5 percent chance of winning the lottery for the No. 1 overall pick. With Cleveland's luck, however, few would have been shocked if a team with a better record saw one of their Ping-Pong balls bounce the winning way.

The tension mounted in Secaucus, New Jersey, as the envelopes were opened in reverse order. With two remaining, the Cavaliers' name had not been revealed. One of the top two picks would be theirs; the other envelope contained Memphis' name but would belong to Detroit via a trade. When NBA Deputy Commissioner Russ Granik announced that the No. 2 pick read "Memphis," cheers bounced off the walls of sports bars throughout the Buckeye state. It was true: Cleveland would pick first in the 2003 NBA Draft.

"It's Christmas in May!" shouted twenty-five-year-old Brian Gannon from his spot at a draft lottery party in Valley View, Ohio.[1] Added Lakewood's John Lewis: "Flat-out unbelievable. [James] is a Cleveland kid and he's going to be staying here. This is going to change the Cleveland market based on one guy being picked. It's about time we had a break go our way. I'm a lot bigger basketball fan now than I was a half-hour ago."[2]

James was not only a local product, having starred in nearby Akron. The six-foot eight-inch sensation was also the most hyped high school athlete in recent history. He averaged more than 30 points and nearly 10 rebounds per game as a senior. Some of his games were shown on national cable television, and he had just signed a $90 million endorsement contract with sporting goods giant Nike.

Home, James

The Official Site of LeBron James offers news, the latest stats, a biography of James, and audio and video clips of the superstar. You can also read his online journal and visit the fan forum.

EDITOR'S CHOICE

James led St. Vincent-St. Mary High School to three state championships in four years. The Associated Press named him Ohio's Mr. Basketball in each of his final three seasons. He also won MVP honors at three of the top 2003 national All-Star games: the McDonald's All American High School Basketball Game, the EA Sports Roundball Classic, and the Jordan Capital Classic. Yes, he would be skipping college, but there was little doubt James was ready for the big time.

▲ Gordon Gund (left), the long-time owner of the Cleveland Cavaliers, holds up a No. 23 LeBron James jersey. He posed for this photo with NBA Deputy Commissioner Russ Granik.

LeBron James would have packed arenas anywhere, of course, but he seemed genuinely delighted that his travels would not take him far from his hometown. "I'm not going to guarantee a championship," he said upon learning the news, surrounded by his high school teammates. "But I will guarantee we'll get better every day. We're going to be a lot better than we were last year."[3]

The lottery victory made team owner Gordon Gund giddy. After earning the No. 1 selection, he stepped to the podium in Secaucus and proclaimed, "We don't know who we are going to pick."[4] Laughter erupted. Everyone in the room knew who the Cavs would select. A smiling Gund later confirmed it by hoisting a wine- and gold-colored Cavaliers jersey with the name James and the No. 23 embroidered on the back. "I'm very excited for the fans of Cleveland," he said. "This is a great day for them and for all of that market, for Akron, Cleveland, all of northeastern Ohio. I'm tremendously excited about it. It's a big day in Cleveland sports."[5]

Cavaliers forward Jim Cleamons looks to stop Dave Bing of the Washington Bullets. This playoff game was played on April 23, 1976.

FITCH'S FRANCHISE

Professional basketball was not new to Cleveland when the Cavaliers joined the National Basketball Association in 1970. In fact, the town was one of pro basketball's true originals. The Cleveland Rebels were among eleven clubs in the Basketball Association of America (BAA), a predecessor of the NBA, in 1946. The Rebels played just one season, but it was an interesting one. The team featured aging hook-shot artist Ed Sadowski. One of the guards, Frankie Baumholtz, was in pro basketball for only that season before beginning a ten-year career in Major League Baseball.

Against those odds in 1946–47, the Rebels made the playoffs by finishing third in the Western Division behind the Chicago Stags and St. Louis Bombers. Sadowski led the team in scoring with 16 points per game. Baumholtz was second with a 14-point average for a team that won half of its sixty games. The success was short-lived, however. The Rebels were beaten by the New York Knickerbockers in the first round of the playoffs. They folded before the start of the BAA's second season.

Steinbrenner's Pipers

Pro basketball returned to Cleveland in 1961. George Steinbrenner (the future New York Yankees owner) was among the founding fathers of the American Basketball League (ABL). The ABL was a collection of the top clubs from the National Alliance of Basketball Leagues and the Amateur Athletic Union. From the latter organization came Steinbrenner's Cleveland Pipers.

The Pipers had won the AAU championship in 1960–61 and quickly became the class of the ABL in 1961–62. John McClendon was the team's initial bench boss, becoming the first African-American head coach of a pro basketball team. He resigned before the Pipers won the league's inaugural championship. The reason: Steinbrenner was interfering in coaching decisions, just like he later would with the baseball Yankees.

Former Boston Celtics standout Bill Sharman took over for McClendon. He inherited a strong squad. Dick Barnett averaged 26.2 points per game and Johnny Cox tossed in 18.5 points,

▲ Jerry Lucas poses as a member of the Cincinnati Royals. George Steinbrenner signed Lucas to play for the Cleveland Pipers. When the Pipers were not allowed into the NBA, the team folded and Lucas moved on.

MyReportLinks.com Books

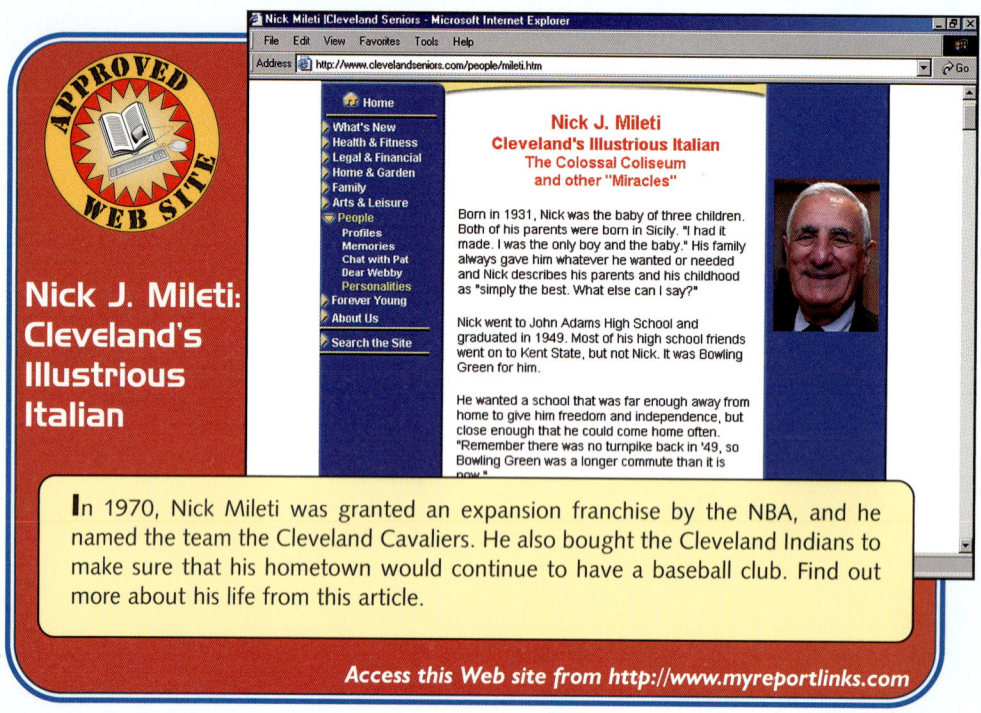

Nick J. Mileti: Cleveland's Illustrious Italian

In 1970, Nick Mileti was granted an expansion franchise by the NBA, and he named the team the Cleveland Cavaliers. He also bought the Cleveland Indians to make sure that his hometown would continue to have a baseball club. Find out more about his life from this article.

Access this Web site from http://www.myreportlinks.com

helping Cleveland win the East Division with a 24–18 ledger. The Pipers then beat Kansas City, 106–102, in the fifth and deciding game of the championship series.

Like the Rebels before them, the Pipers' glory was short-lived. Although things were looking up when Steinbrenner signed Ohio State All-American Jerry Lucas, he wanted to debut his star player in the NBA—not the ABL. The NBA, however, refused to admit the Pipers. So Steinbrenner disbanded the team prior to the 1962–63 season. Before that campaign came to a close, the financially troubled ABL was history, too.

NBA, Here We Come

Steinbrenner moved on to other endeavors before Cleveland was admitted to the NBA. It was Cleveland native Nick Mileti who made NBA hoops happen in Cleveland. In the wake of a 1969 oil fire on the Cuyahoga River that branded Cleveland as one of the most polluted cities in the country, Mileti helped restore some civic pride. The lawyer-turned-sports baron was granted an NBA expansion franchise in 1970.

Cleveland celebrated. However, if fans had known just how long it would take for their newest pro sports team to be competitive, they might have been more subdued. Mileti hired former University of Minnesota basketball boss Bill Fitch as the team's first head coach and general manager (GM). In a quip that was both memorable and prophetic, the coach told the press: "The name's Fitch; not Houdini."[1] Fitch's inability to work magic began with the expansion draft. The Cavaliers were able to obtain precious little talent from other clubs, patching together a roster of mediocre veterans and unproven youngsters. They were destined to struggle.

Compounding their troubles, the Ice Capades Show was in town for the start of the 1970–71 season. Cleveland Arena, also owned by Mileti, was booked. Thus, the Cavaliers would have to play the first seven games of their existence on the road. The opener was against fellow expansion club Buffalo. It soon became clear which team was better. Buffalo never trailed after taking an early 12–10 edge, en route to a 107–92 runaway. Offered Fitch: "A game like this tells me why show people take their shows on the road before coming home. People may think I'm crazy after seeing how bad we were, but I really believe that before we finish our 12 games with Buffalo we'll be playing them even."[2]

By the end of the seven straight road games, the Cavaliers were 0–7. They had lost those games

The Cavaliers played in the Cleveland Arena until 1974. It was demolished in 1977, and subsequently, the American Red Cross erected a building on the land. A short history of the Arena is provided on the **Cleveland Arena** page.

Fitch's Franchise

by an average of seventeen points. And Buffalo was not too worried about Fitch's prediction.

A Laugher of a Season

Two of the eleven players taken by the Cavaliers in the 1970 expansion draft never wore a Cleveland uniform. Of the other nine, only one—Bobby "Bingo" Smith—would spend more than four years with the club. Of course, no one knew that would be the case when 6,144 curious patrons spun the turnstiles at Cleveland Arena on October 28, 1970. The Cavaliers lost that first home game to San Diego, 110–99.

More misery followed. The Cavaliers started with fifteen losses in a row, including a 141–87 embarrassment at Philadelphia, before they finally won a game. Their first victory came in Portland against a fellow expansion team which, weeks earlier, had defeated Cleveland for its initial win. The rematch went to the Cavaliers, 105–103. Almost a full month into the season, Fitch and his players finally had something to celebrate. It would have to hold them for awhile. They promptly lost their next twelve before posting their first home win against Buffalo.

The Cavaliers were 2–34 at one point during that initial campaign. That is not to say they were not entertaining on their way to a 15–67 mark. During one game, guard Bobby Lewis made an

▲ The newly formed Cleveland Cavaliers selected Austin Carr with the top pick in the 1971 NBA Draft. Carr is shown here during his senior season at the University of Notre Dame.

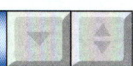

Fitch's Franchise

inbound pass to a wide-open John Warren, who raced toward the wrong basket and scored two points for the opposition. Perhaps almost as comical was the scene around the hoop. Portland's LeRoy Ellis tried to block the shot. Meanwhile, Cleveland's Bobby Smith was hollering for the ball because he, too, was in position to score. "If we can't laugh at ourselves," Fitch once said, "then we're going to get mad when others laugh at us."[3]

No one was laughing on February 19, 1971, although only 3,896 fans got to witness Walt Wesley's historic night at Cleveland Arena. Wesley scored 34 points in the first half of a game against the Cincinnati Royals and finished with 50. The mark would stand as the club record for thirty-five years. Two nights later, Wesley notched the team's first "20–20" game, totaling 30 points and 21 rebounds at Portland. Wesley's 17.7 points per game led the Cavaliers. Rookie John Johnson averaged 16.6 points per game and was the team's first all-star.

A Talent Infusion

It became painfully obvious in that first season that the road to respectability would be a long one for the Cavaliers. Fortunately, help arrived via the 1971 NBA Draft. The selection of college scoring machine Austin Carr with the first overall pick was a terrific start. Carr was virtually unstoppable at the University of Notre Dame. His three-year scoring average of 34.5 points per game ranked among the best in NCAA history. An injury limited Carr to forty-three games during his first season, but he made the NBA All-Rookie Team.

In 1971–72, the Cavaliers recorded their first sellout of Cleveland Arena. During a game in January, more than eleven thousand fans crammed into the building to watch the Cavaliers play the star-studded Los Angeles Lakers. Cleveland's 23–59 record still left them in last

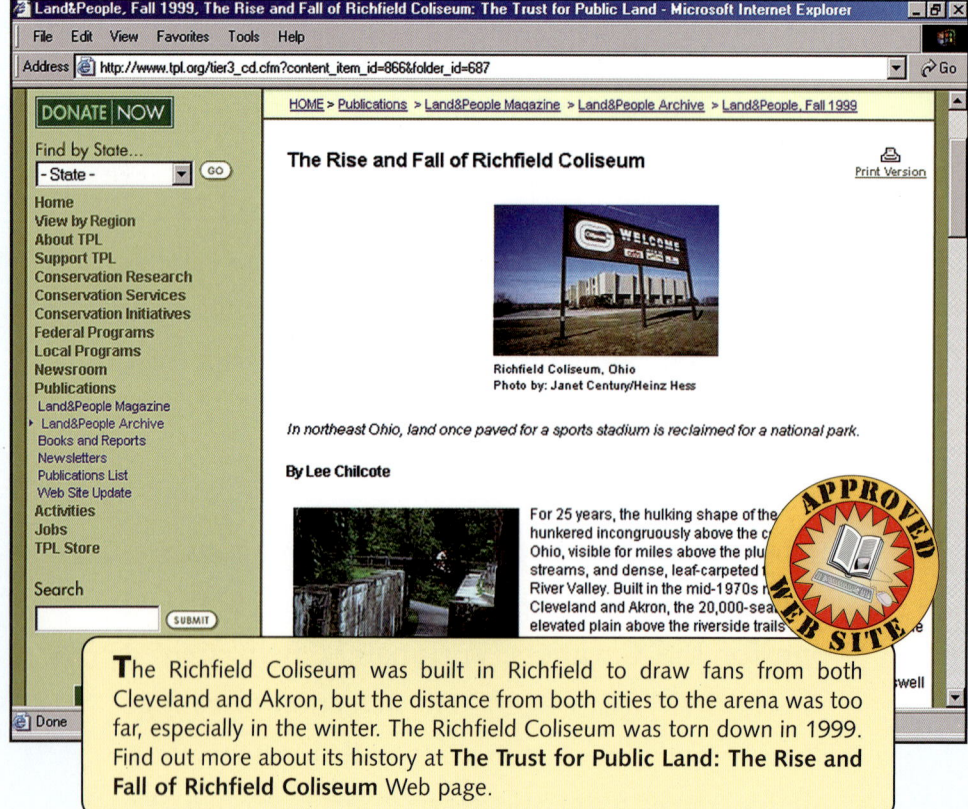

The Richfield Coliseum was built in Richfield to draw fans from both Cleveland and Akron, but the distance from both cities to the arena was too far, especially in the winter. The Richfield Coliseum was torn down in 1999. Find out more about its history at **The Trust for Public Land: The Rise and Fall of Richfield Coliseum** Web page.

Fitch's Franchise

place in the Central Division, but at least there was a glimmer of hope. After the season, the Cavs traded All-Star Alfred "Butch" Beard to Seattle for Barry Clemens and a man who would mean as much to the franchise as anyone in the coming years—point guard Lenny Wilkens.

In 1972–73, Wilkens finished second in the NBA with 8.4 assists per game. The team won six straight games during one stretch and finished at 32–50. The next season, Cleveland slumped to 29 victories for its fourth straight last-place finish. Nevertheless, the pieces were in place for a run at respectability.

That emergence began the following season—in a new location. Many criticized Mileti's decision to take the Cavaliers away from downtown and out to the suburbs. But the new, 19,500-seat Richfield Coliseum was a considerable upgrade over Cleveland Arena. In 1974–75, the Cavs won 40 games and finished out of last place for the first time. The final home game that year attracted 20,239 fans.

All We Need Is a Miracle

In their second season in the new building, the Cavaliers pulled off the "Miracle of Richfield." Truth be told, it really was not a miracle at all. Fitch had steadily built a playoff-caliber team that had as much depth as any club in the NBA. A trade that brought Jim Chones from Los Angeles helped put the Cavaliers over the top. Chones led the club in scoring with 15.8 points per game in that magical 1975–76 season, but he was just one of seven players to average double figures in scoring. "We all know our roles," said reserve Nate Thurmond. "Everybody knows he's going to get his minutes and do his thing. That's why we have such a beautiful machine."[4]

Cleveland went 49–33 to edge Washington by one game for the Central Division title. It was the team's first playoff berth, and gave them home

The greatest moment in Cavaliers early history was forged at the Richfield Coliseum during the 1975–76 season. **Cavaliers History: The Making of a Miracle** is an overview of the Washington Bullets versus Cavaliers series.

Fitch's Franchise

court advantage in the subsequent playoff series with the Washington Bullets. Fitch was named NBA Coach of the Year. The Cavaliers achieved even greater success in the postseason, when they squared off against the division rival Bullets in the first round.

Washington's opening win in Richfield stole home-court advantage from the Cavaliers. In Game 2, the Bullets held a one-point lead and had possession in the closing moments, but Cleveland forced a turnover with six seconds to go. Then Bingo Smith tossed in a rainbow jump shot for an 80–79 victory. The series was even.

How About Three?

It was the first of three "miracle" finishes in the series. Game 5 saw Jim Cleamons grab a missed shot in midair, then spin it over his head and through the hoop for a 92–91 Cavaliers victory. But the greatest of those nail-biters came in the decisive Game 7 before a record 21,564 fans at the Coliseum. With the score tied, the Cavaliers' Dick Snyder caught an inbound pass from Cleamons and raced past Bullets star Wes Unseld. Snyder banked a shot high off the glass and through the hoop with four seconds remaining. When a last-second attempt from the corner by Washington's Phil Chenier missed its mark, the Cavaliers had earned an 87–85 decision to win their first-ever playoff series.

MyReportLinks.com Books

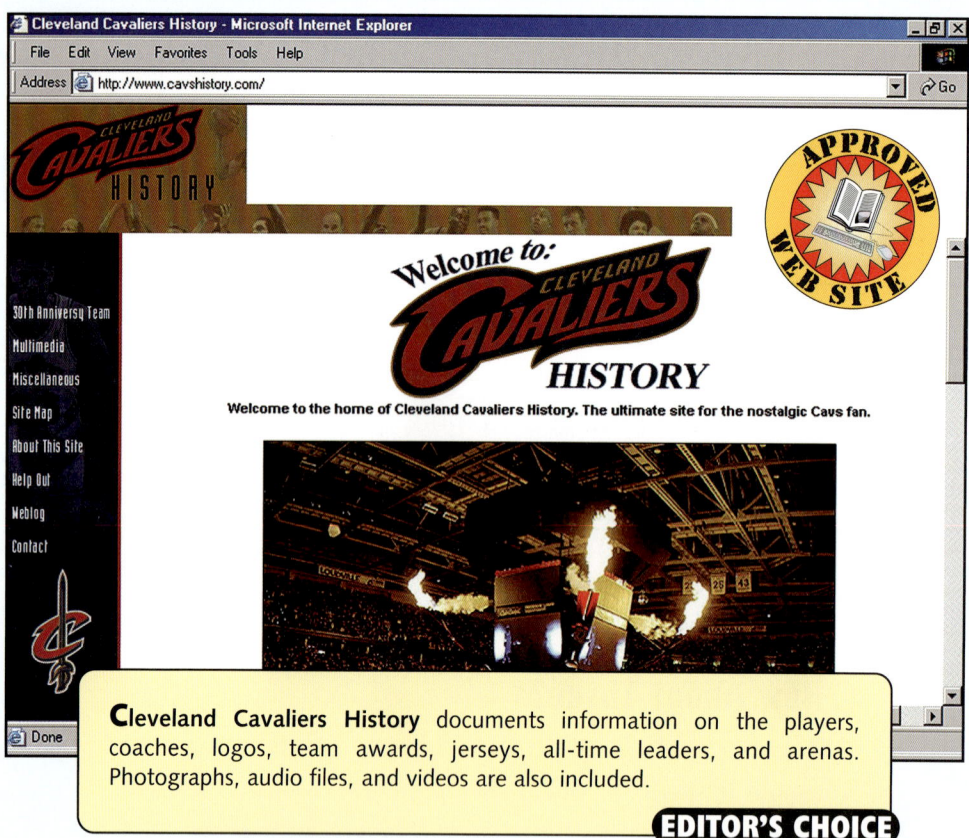

Cleveland Cavaliers History documents information on the players, coaches, logos, team awards, jerseys, all-time leaders, and arenas. Photographs, audio files, and videos are also included.

EDITOR'S CHOICE

Cleveland was eliminated by the Boston Celtics in six games in the Conference Finals, but the "Miracle of Richfield" had given Cavs fans something to hang their hats on: memorable moments; late-game heroics; poise under pressure; and perhaps most important, hope for the future. No one would have believed it would take sixteen years for the team to win its second playoff series.

Back to Earth

Though the Cavaliers' rise to conference finalist was a slow climb, their fall from contention was more abrupt. They won their first eight games in 1976–77, but their 43–39 record fell six games short of their previous season's achievement. Washington eliminated them in the first round of playoffs. The following season produced an identical record and a second straight first-round loss, this time to the New York Knicks. Not even a trade that secured future Hall of Famer Walt Frazier could push the Cavs over the top.

Fitch Resigns

By the 1978–79 season, it became obvious that the Cavaliers were not about to recapture their "Miracle" magic. Michael "Campy" Russell averaged more than 20 points per game. Carr, Chones, Smith, and rookie Mike Mitchell also filled the nets. But only one team in the NBA was faring worse defensively than the Cavaliers. Cleveland's opponents averaged 110.2 points per game, and as a result the Cavs finished 30–52. On May 21, 1979, after nine seasons, Fitch announced his resignation. Two days later, he was hired to coach the Boston Celtics, with whom he would win an NBA championship.

Stan Albeck took over as Cleveland's second head coach. His first season included one of the more dramatic games in franchise history. On January 29, 1980, the Cavaliers and Los Angeles Lakers played a quadruple-overtime thriller at the

Coliseum. Lakers guard Norm Nixon played an NBA-record sixty-four minutes. Cleveland won, 154–153, the highlight of an otherwise forgettable 37–45 season.

Coaching Carousel

For awhile in 1983, it looked as though the Cavaliers might be forced to leave northeast Ohio. The team was not faring well in the standings or at the gate for owner Ted Stepien, who had made a series of bad trades and poor draft selections. A move was discussed, but brothers George and Gordon Gund came to the rescue. Co-owners of the Coliseum, the Gunds agreed to purchase the team in April 1983 and keep it in Cleveland. The NBA felt so sorry for the way the Cavaliers had been managed that the league's board of governors awarded the team a bonus first-round draft pick for each of the next four years.

Eventually, those picks would help. In the short term, however, the Cavaliers could not even find a proper coach. From 1979–80 through 1985–86, the club saw eight different head coaches draw up plays. Albeck was replaced after one season by Bill Musselman, who in less than a year was replaced by General Manager Don Delaney. Both Musselman and Delaney coached part of the following (1981–82) campaign, too, as did Bob Kloppenburg and Chuck Daly. Tom Nissalke was

Fitch's Franchise

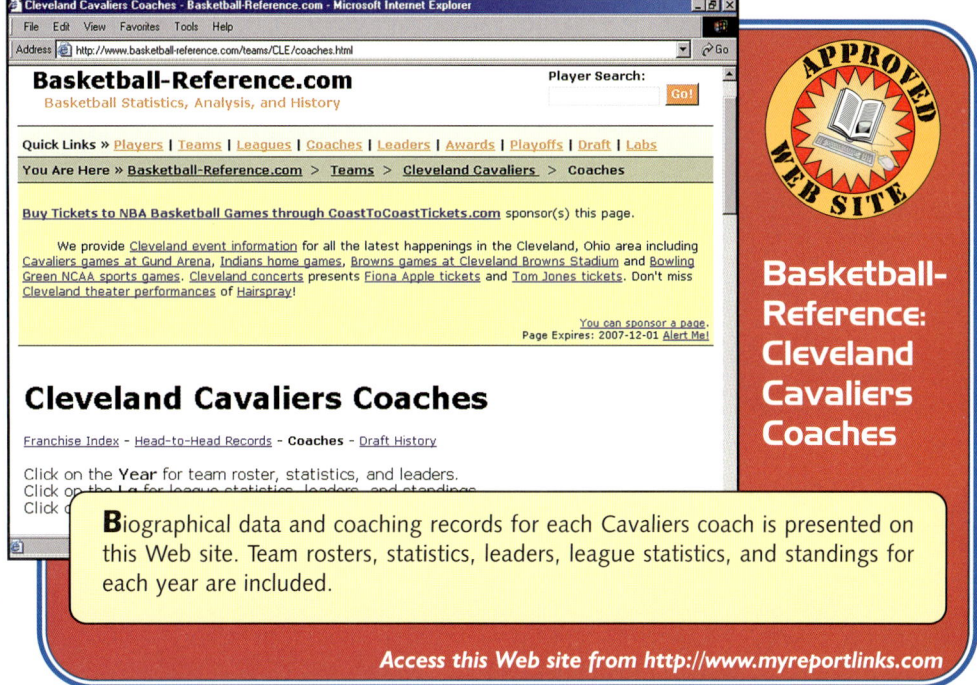

Basketball-Reference: Cleveland Cavaliers Coaches

Biographical data and coaching records for each Cavaliers coach is presented on this Web site. Team rosters, statistics, leaders, league statistics, and standings for each year are included.

Access this Web site from http://www.myreportlinks.com

named coach a mere week before the 1982–83 season—who needs preparation time?—and actually lasted two seasons. In 1984–85, George Karl overcame a 2–19 start and took the Cavs to the playoffs. By the end of the following season, Karl was gone. So, too, was interim replacement Gene Littles after just fifteen games.

▲ *This photo from the 1992 Eastern Conference Finals shows the Bulls' Horace Grant challenging the shot of Cavs legend Larry Nance. Nance was chosen as a starting forward on Cleveland's 30th Anniversary All-Time Team.*

TITLE CONTENDER 3

Cleveland, home of the Rock and Roll Hall of Fame and Museum, loves its music. Until the summer of 1986, its basketball team seemed stuck with a bad case of the blues. Then, in the span of just a few weeks, the beat picked up thanks to some good fortune and wise decisions.

The Cavaliers were without a general manager and head coach in the weeks leading up to the 1986 NBA Draft. Given their success in that year's distribution of talent, perhaps it is a formula more teams should try! The Philadelphia 76ers had the No. 1 choice in that draft, but they were looking for immediate help from a veteran. So they traded the top pick to Cleveland for forward Roy Hinson and cash.

Philadelphia was enamored with Hinson's athletic talent and the scoring ability he displayed over his three seasons with Cleveland. Hinson had become a starter as a rookie, tallied 15.8 points per game in his second season, and averaged just under 20 points per game in 1985–86. The 76ers felt that Hinson might help them recapture some of the magic that had produced an NBA championship in 1983. They also believed that no one in the 1986 NBA Draft could make a big impact.

Pivotal Draft Picks

In particular, there were doubts about North Carolina center Brad Daugherty as a potential top choice. Some thought he might be too "soft" to star in the NBA. Without a general manager or head coach, the Cavaliers' ownership relied on the advice of their scouts. They saw Daugherty as a perfect fit for a team that needed a center who could score. The Cavaliers used the No. 1 pick on the big man. Before long, the trade became known as one of the most one-sided deals in NBA history. The oft-injured Hinson never matched his third-year scoring pace, and Daugherty emerged as a five-time All-Star.

It was not the Cavaliers' only draft-day victory of 1986. In fact, they were the big winners. After Daugherty, they drafted Ron Harper, who would average 22.9 points per game as a rookie. They also landed Mark Price (in a trade from Dallas), who would serve as the team's starting point

▲ The Cavs' Johnny Davis attempts a finger-roll over the outstretched arms of Eric Floyd of the Golden State Warriors.

guard for nearly a decade and set the NBA's career free-throw accuracy record. Finally, they landed Johnny Newman, who would play sixteen seasons in the NBA. The Cavs secured the services of four players who should have been among the first fifteen players drafted that year.

Leadership Arrives

Owner Gordon Gund called it "probably the most pivotal week in franchise history."[1] Within days of the 1986 draft, Cleveland filled its leadership void. Wayne Embry, who in 1972 had become the NBA's first African-American general manager with the Milwaukee Bucks, became GM and vice president of the Cavs. And three weeks later, Embry hired another African American, former Cavs star Lenny Wilkens, to coach the team.

The bountiful draft sparked optimism about the 1986–87 season. "I'm excited about the young talent there," said the forty-eight-year-old Wilkens, who had guided Seattle to an NBA championship in 1979. "I know they're not going to win right away; it's going to take some time, but they had a fine draft this year."[2] An additional piece of the puzzle, swingman Craig Ehlo, was signed as a free agent during the season. Although Cleveland finished 31–51, the future looked bright. Three straight winning seasons would follow.

▲ Cavaliers head coach Lenny Wilkens was also a great point guard for Cleveland during his playing days. Wilkens was inducted into the Basketball Hall of Fame as both a player and coach.

MyReportLinks.com Books

Two of those next three winning seasons would produce 42–40 records. But it was the campaign in between—the 1988–89 season—that Cavaliers fans will never forget. Wilkens was named coach of the Eastern Conference All-Star Team. Price, Daugherty, and shot-blocking specialist Larry Nance all made that All-Star squad. And Nance became the first player in franchise history to be named to the NBA All-Defensive First Team.

It was not those individual milestones, or a 57–25 record, that fans remember most about the 1988–89 Cavaliers. It was one jump shot—"The Shot," as it became known in Cleveland—in

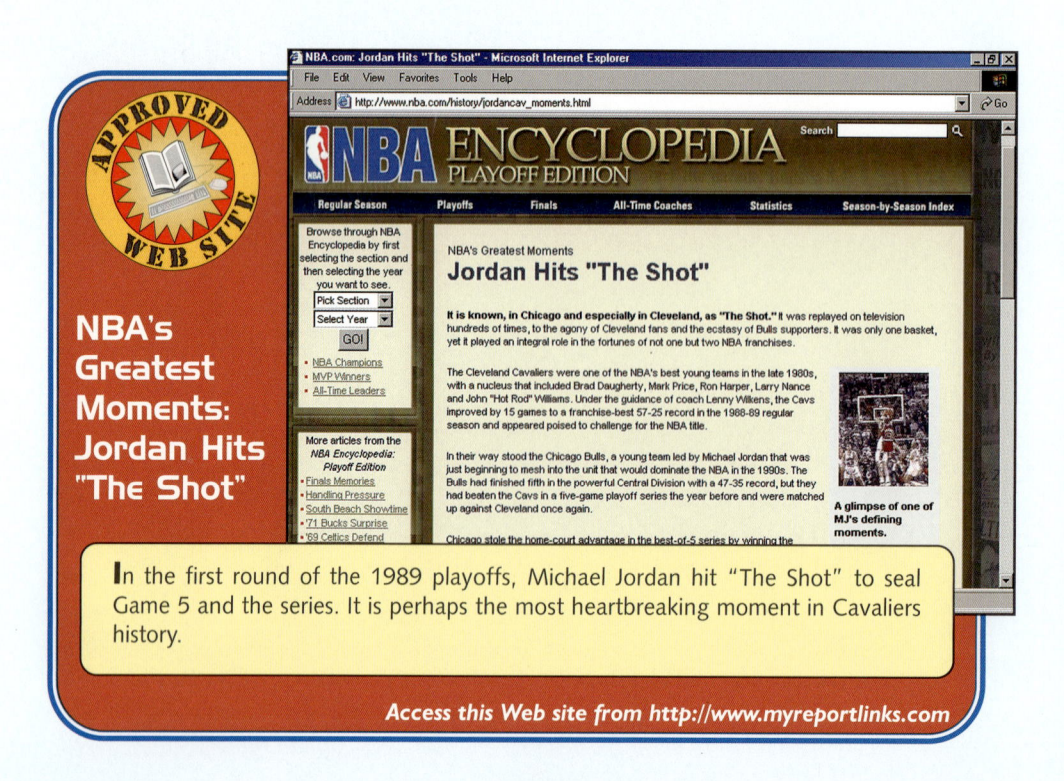

NBA's Greatest Moments: Jordan Hits "The Shot"

In the first round of the 1989 playoffs, Michael Jordan hit "The Shot" to seal Game 5 and the series. It is perhaps the most heartbreaking moment in Cavaliers history.

Access this Web site from http://www.myreportlinks.com

Title Contender

the first round of the playoffs that forever defined this powerful Cavs team.

"The Shot"

The Cavaliers had defeated Michael Jordan and the Chicago Bulls six consecutive times during the regular season. That was the main reason folks were scratching their heads when Jordan predicted the Bulls would win their playoff series. Even when Chicago pushed the set to a deciding fifth game, fans still believed the Cavs would avenge the previous year's first-round loss to Chicago.

It came down to the final seconds. Ehlo had given Cleveland a 100–99 lead and sent the Coliseum crowd into a frenzy with a driving, two-handed layup. "The layup seemed to be the period to end the sentence," Ehlo recalled.[3] All the Cavs needed was a defensive stop in the final three seconds. Their defensive task was an obvious one, as everyone in the arena knew which Chicago player would get the ball.

Before Chicago's Brad Sellers inbounded the ball, Ehlo and Nance blanketed Jordan near the hoop. They then recovered in time to resume the effort after the Bulls guard had zipped out to the free-throw line. As Sellers pump-faked a pass elsewhere, he spotted Jordan breaking free from his two defenders on the right wing. The ball went to Jordan.

What happened next remains one of the most replayed highlights in sports. Jordan dribbled toward the top of the key as an off-balance Ehlo tried to knock the ball away. Jordan pulled up from just inside the circle. Ehlo went up, too, reaching for a piece of the ball. Jordan, hanging in the air, pulled the ball away from Ehlo's outstretched fingertips and managed to launch his shot—"The Shot"—all in one motion. It rattled in. Jordan jumped again in celebration, adding three unforgettable fist pumps for good measure. The Bulls won, 101–100, on their way

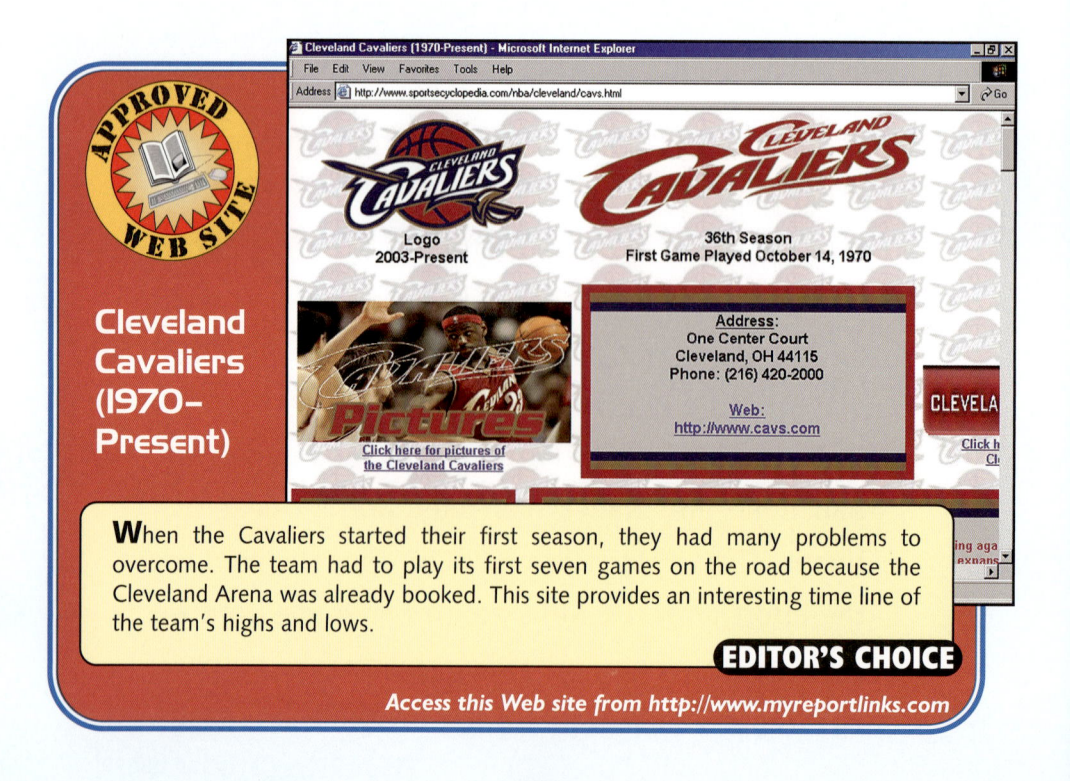

Cleveland Cavaliers (1970–Present)

When the Cavaliers started their first season, they had many problems to overcome. The team had to play its first seven games on the road because the Cleveland Arena was already booked. This site provides an interesting time line of the team's highs and lows.

EDITOR'S CHOICE

Access this Web site from http://www.myreportlinks.com

Title Contender

to emerging as an NBA dynasty for the better part of a decade.

Meanwhile, Cleveland was left to ponder what might have been. "We jumped at the same time," Ehlo said years later, "but I came down a lot quicker than him."[4] The same can be said of the Cavaliers. They won fifteen fewer games the following year and lost in the first round of the playoffs to Philadelphia. In 1990–91, they tumbled to 33–49.

"Yes, Virginia, There Is a Santa Claus"

Ehlo was involved in another memorable shot three seasons after his unsuccessful duel with Jordan. On December 23, 1991, his three-pointer at the buzzer beat Utah in a hard-fought regular-season game. It was a clutch shot, to be sure. However, it was the call of longtime Cleveland radio voice Joe Tait that took on a life of its own in northeast Ohio.

"Yes, Virginia, there is a Santa Claus," Tait shouted into his microphone, "and he comes from Lubbock, Texas!" Explained Tait years later, "To this day I don't have a clue where it came from . . . it just popped out!"[5]

If Tait's "Santa Claus" call was a gift for Cavaliers fans, the team itself treated its followers to a marvelous season. Cleveland finished 57–25 in 1991–92, good for second place in the Central

MyReportLinks.com Books

Division. One of those regular-season wins was a 148–80 romp over Miami, the most lopsided victory in franchise history. It was the Cavaliers' long-awaited success in the postseason, however, that marked the most significant progress.

The first round of the playoffs had become the annual "end of the road" for Cleveland. Not this year. The Cavaliers won their first postseason series since 1976 when they defeated New Jersey in the first round, three games to one. Up next were Larry Bird and the Celtics. The Cavaliers won the opener at home, but Boston took the next two, stealing home-court advantage. Behind 32 points from Nance, the Cavaliers earned back that edge with a 114–112 overtime thriller at the Boston

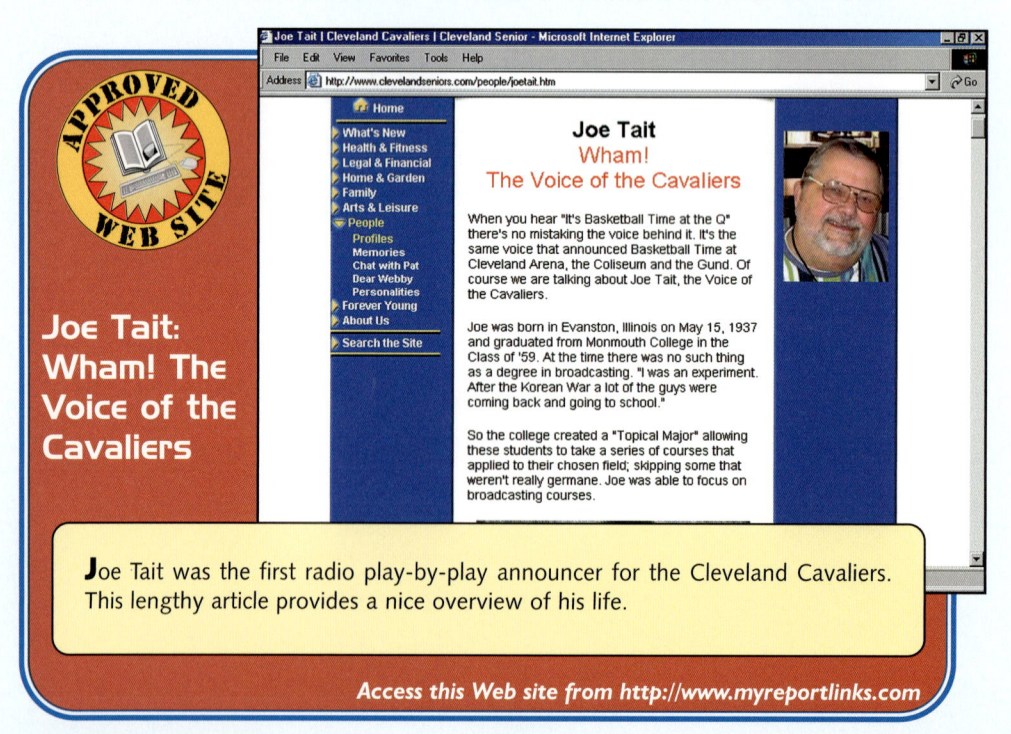

Joe Tait: Wham! The Voice of the Cavaliers

Joe Tait was the first radio play-by-play announcer for the Cleveland Cavaliers. This lengthy article provides a nice overview of his life.

Access this Web site from http://www.myreportlinks.com

Garden. The series was knotted at two games apiece.

The series reached a deciding Game 7 at the Coliseum. As it turned out, it was not much of a game at all. Six Cavaliers reached double figures in scoring in a 122–104 rout. For the first time in franchise history, the Cavaliers had won two playoff series in the same year. But once again, Chicago proved to be Cleveland's downfall. The Bulls knocked out the Cavs in the Eastern Conference Finals, winning four games to two.

The More Things Change . . .

Wilkens steered the Cavaliers to a 54–28 record in 1992–93 in his final season as the team's coach. It marked the first time in history that the club put together back-to-back fifty-win campaigns, and Mark Price became the first Cavalier to make the All-NBA First Team. But Jordan and Chicago defeated the Cavaliers in the Eastern Conference Semifinals. As such, Cleveland became known as the team that could not "get over the hump." Wilkens resigned, and Mike Fratello came aboard as coach.

Fratello's first season was the team's last one in Richfield. The outcome was familiar. A 47–35 record was good for a third-place divisional finish, and the Bulls took care of the rest. This time, it was a first-round sweep.

Something had to change, and it did. The Cavaliers unveiled new uniforms during the summer before the 1994–95 season, although some might argue that "new" did not necessarily mean "improved." A diagonal and somewhat electric look replaced the classic ball-through-net "V" on the old Cavs jerseys. The team also moved to Gund Arena, a multipurpose facility in downtown Cleveland.

Unfortunately, new uniforms and a new home did not translate into playoff success. Despite tying a franchise record with 11 successive wins,

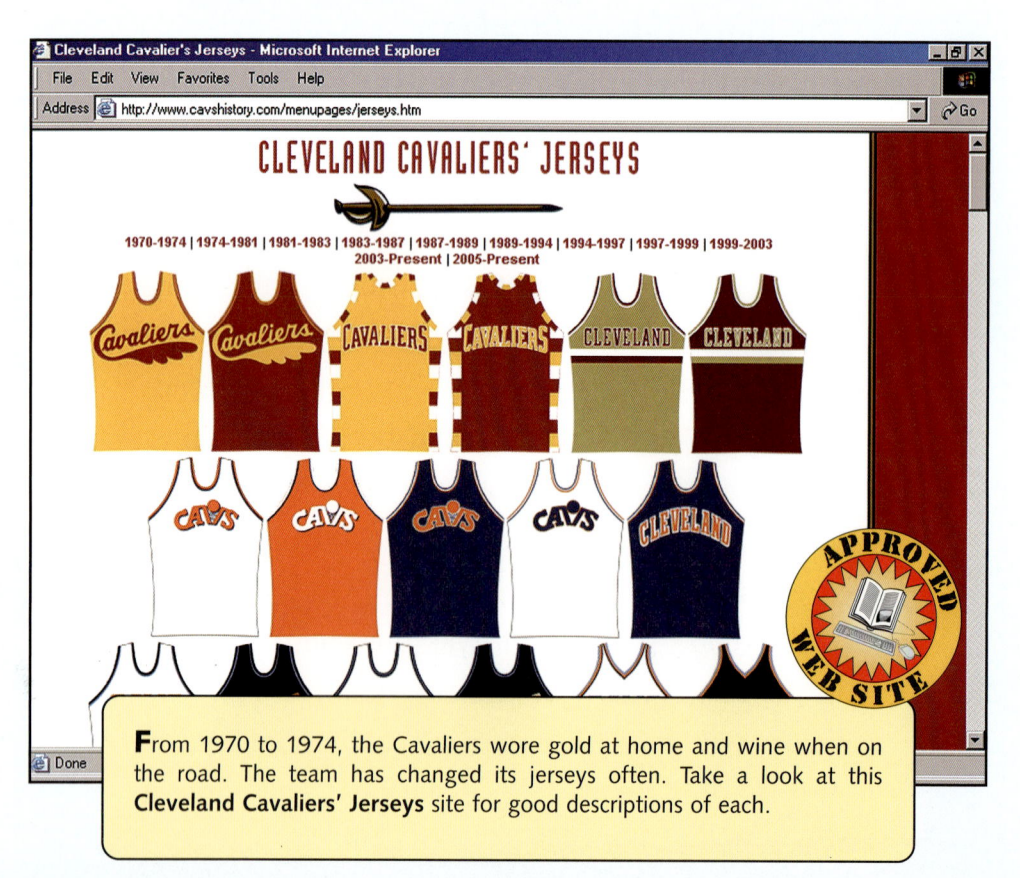

From 1970 to 1974, the Cavaliers wore gold at home and wine when on the road. The team has changed its jerseys often. Take a look at this **Cleveland Cavaliers' Jerseys** site for good descriptions of each.

Title Contender

Cleveland followed a decent 43–39 season with a first-round loss to the Knicks. Fratello's bunch improved to 47–35 in 1995–96, marking the Cavaliers' fifth consecutive winning season and trip to the playoffs. This time, their first-round loss to the Knicks came via a three-game sweep.

The playoff streak ended in 1996–97, when a 42–40 ledger had Cleveland on the outside looking in. By then, the lineup was vastly different from the one that had been victimized by the Bulls for so many years. Daugherty had retired. So, too, had Price, leaving the point guard role in the hands of Terrell Brandon. The up-and-comer led the team in scoring with 19.5 points per game. Meanwhile, Tyrone Hill replaced Nance as the club's big-rebounding all-star forward.

In the Midst of Greatness

Not even the Rock and Roll Hall of Fame could hold a candle to this assemblage of talent. During the 1997 NBA All-Star Weekend in Cleveland, the league rolled out its "50 Greatest Players in NBA History." It was a collection of greats that had combined to produce 107 NBA championships, 49 Most Valuable Player Awards, 447 All-Star Game selections, 36 scoring titles, and nearly one million points.

Wilkens was among them, giving the home folks a local favorite. The top fifty players were chosen by a panel of media, former players and coaches, and current and former GMs and executives. It was a proud moment for the NBA, which had come a long way over five decades. Cleveland fans hoped that some of that progress might rub off on the Cavaliers, who were, in some ways, still trying to overcome "The Shot."

Mike Fratello's final two seasons on the bench were a study in contrast. The Cavaliers put a strong team on the floor in 1997–98. Forward Shawn Kemp became the first Cleveland player voted to start in the All-Star Game. Four Cavs youngsters—Brevin Knight, Zydrunas Ilgauskas, Derek Anderson, and Cedric Henderson—made either the first or second NBA All-Rookie Team.

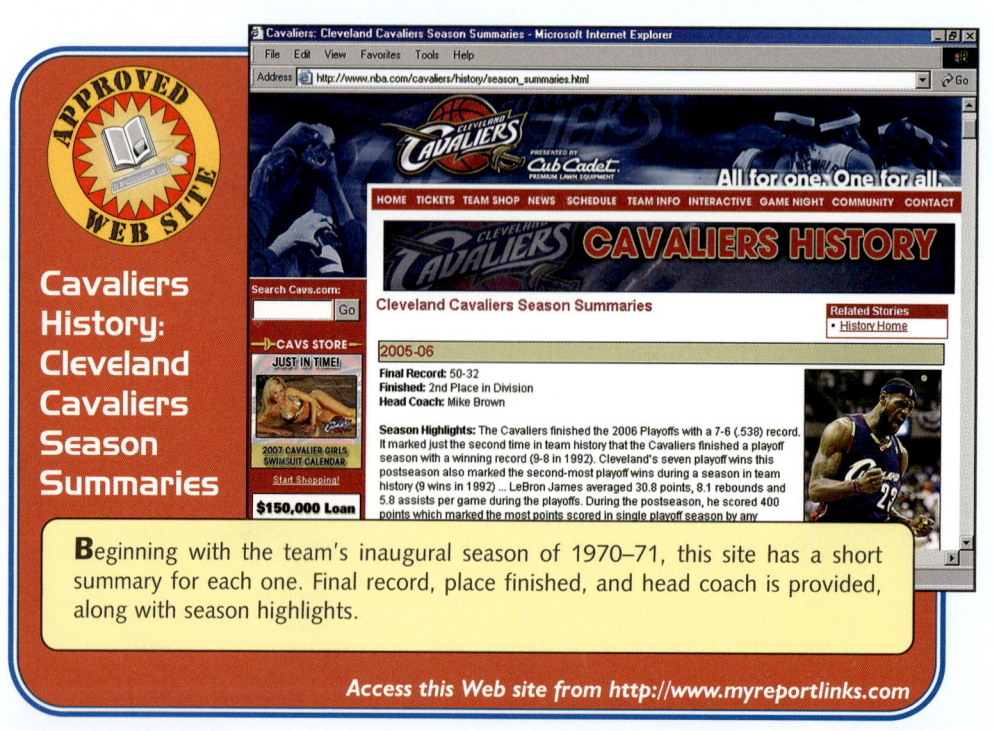

Cavaliers History: Cleveland Cavaliers Season Summaries

Beginning with the team's inaugural season of 1970–71, this site has a short summary for each one. Final record, place finished, and head coach is provided, along with season highlights.

Access this Web site from http://www.myreportlinks.com

Moreover, The *Sporting News* named Wayne Embry its NBA Executive of the Year after his club finished 47–35. Unfortunately, another first-round loss awaited the Cavs, this time at the hands of the Indiana Pacers.

A Team in Transition

That season marked a crossroads for the Cavaliers. A labor impasse delayed the start of the following campaign until February 1999. If Cleveland was a disappointment in the 1998 playoffs, it was an even bigger one the next winter. The Cavs won only 22 of 50 games. Under new executive Jim Paxson, who would be promoted to GM in June 1999, a coaching change was made. Out went Fratello. In came former NBA journeyman Randy Wittman for his first head coaching job at age thirty-nine. Wittman had been a bright and highly respected assistant with the Pacers, Mavericks, and Timberwolves. He was expected to reinvigorate a Cavs team whose fortunes and attendance had taken a plunge.

In reality, leading Cleveland to any kind of dramatic turnaround would have been too tall an order for even the most experienced NBA coaches. The Cavaliers featured some promising young players, but no one was ready to carry the franchise to new heights. More rough seasons lay ahead.

▲ *Shawn Kemp was traded to the Cleveland Cavaliers prior to the 1997–98 season. He played only three seasons for the Cavs, but is considered one of the best players in team history.*

Little to Celebrate

The Cavaliers "celebrated" the team's thirtieth anniversary in 1999–2000. An all-time Cleveland starting five was selected, featuring three players who had taken the club to its greatest success. Point guard Mark Price led the way, along with big men Larry Nance and Brad Daugherty. The other selections "bookended" that trio—Austin Carr from the early era, and Shawn Kemp from the current one.

The Cavaliers went 32–50 in their first season under Coach Wittman, then slipped to 30–52 in 2000–01. Another former NBA player, John Lucas, replaced Wittman the following year, but the club's slide continued. His first team won just 29 games, and his second season started 8–34. Lucas was relieved of his duties on January 20, 2003, and interim head coach Keith Smart finished up a dismal 17–65 campaign.

If ever a team needed help, it was this one. The organization was willing to try just about anything. The franchise changed the team colors, the uniforms, the logo, and the court design at Gund Arena following that forgettable 2002–03 slate. However, the most significant improvement in franchise history was lurking right around the corner, in Akron. His name was LeBron James.

Flying through the air, LeBron James is about to complete a reverse slam against the Detroit Pistons.

THE KING JAMES ERA

Cleveland's triumph in the 2003 NBA Draft Lottery energized a franchise like no victory on the court ever could. Gund Arena staff could barely keep up with ticket demand after James was drafted. In June of that year, James played his last home-state high school game at Gund, earning MVP honors with 27 points in the McDonald's All American High School Basketball Game.

Earlier in his senior season at St. Vincent-St. Mary, James struck for 31 points in a nationally televised win over Oak Hill Academy at the Cleveland State Convocation Center. Clearly, Cleveland fans knew they were getting someone special—a once-in-decades talent who could dominate immediately in the NBA, despite jumping straight from the high school ranks.

On October 29, 2003, "King James" began his NBA career at the Arco Arena in Sacramento. The game certainly did not have the feel of the usual regular-season opener. More than three hundred media members were on hand, along with the television cameras of ESPN, which aired the game nationally. In the opening quarter, James pumped in 12 points and made 3 steals in a four-possession stretch. He turned one of those swipes into a one-handed slam dunk that instantly became desktop wallpaper material. James finished with 25 points, 9 assists, 6 rebounds, 4 steals, and instant respect.

"It Was for Real"

"He's the real deal," Sacramento center Vlade Divac said of the eighteen year old after the Kings' 106–92 win.[1] The game drew a higher television rating than all but one of ESPN's sixty-nine regular-season telecasts from the previous season.

The impact was felt at the Cavaliers' box office. A second wave of fans rushed to gobble up seats for home games for a Cavs club that had already tripled its season-ticket base. "Obviously, people have been excited," Cavaliers President Len Komoroski said after James's debut. "But I think there were some waiting to see if it was for real. I think a lot of those questions have been answered."[2]

The Cavaliers lost fifteen of their first nineteen games, despite the energy generated by James. They played close to .500 basketball thereafter,

The King James Era

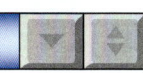

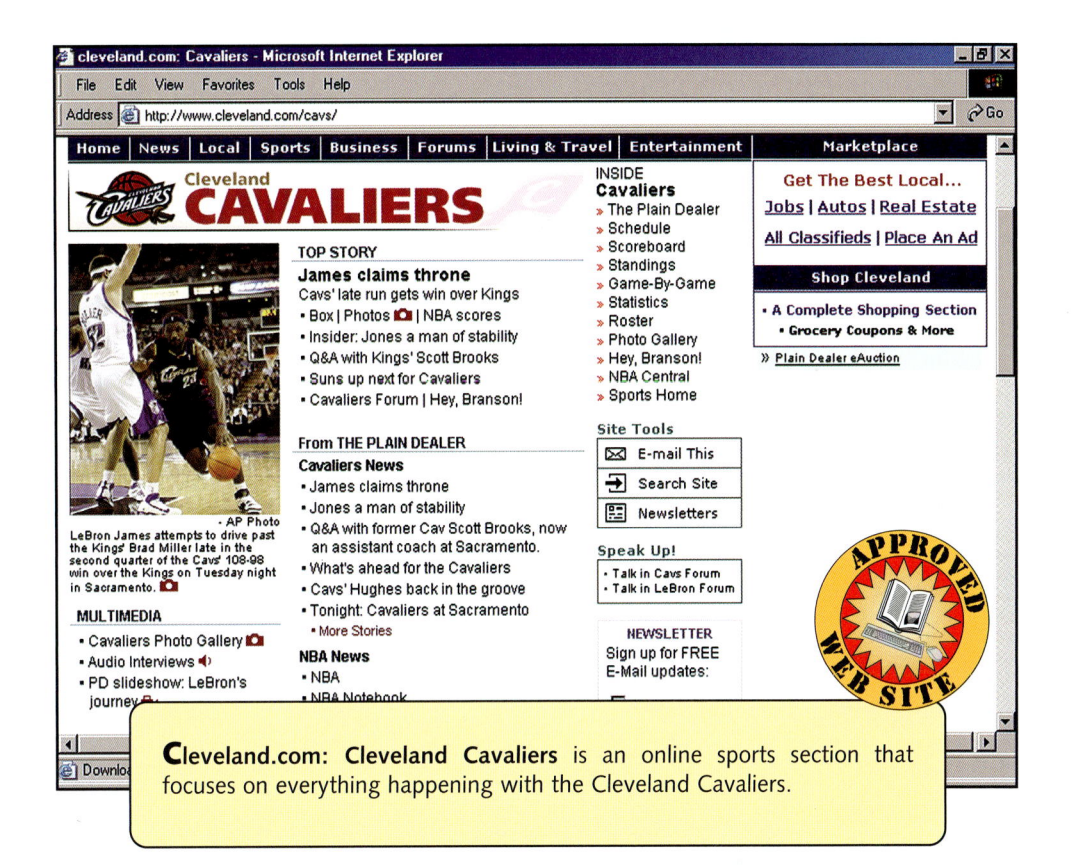

Cleveland.com: Cleveland Cavaliers is an online sports section that focuses on everything happening with the Cleveland Cavaliers.

and finished with 35 wins—18 more than the previous season. James earned NBA Rookie of the Year honors after joining Oscar Robertson and Michael Jordan as the only rookies ever to average at least 20 points, 5 assists, and 5 rebounds per game. He was not Cleveland's only bright spot. Carlos Boozer became the first Cavs player since 1994–95 to average a double-double (15.5 points, 11.4 rebounds per game).

Things were looking up in the front office, too. LeBron James jerseys were flying off shelves across America, and Cleveland's attendance made a record jump. Its home average of 18,288 fans was an increase of 6,791 over the 2002–03 season—the largest one-season leap in NBA history. The Cavaliers sold out thirty-three of forty-one road games and ten of their last fourteen at home.

Tripling His Fun

It soon became clear that Cavaliers basketball could now be split into two distinct eras—before LeBron James (B.L.) and after LeBron James (A.L.). Year 2 A.L. featured several impressive firsts for James and saw a return to winning basketball for the Cavaliers. They finished 42–40 in 2004–05 under head coaches Paul Silas and Brendan Malone. Cleveland fell just one game short of qualifying for the playoffs.

James's play, which was drawing favorable comparisons to that of Michael Jordan, soared to another level on January 19, 2005. That is when he became the youngest player ever to record a triple-double. His 27 points, 11 rebounds, and 10 assists led the Cavaliers to a 107–101 win over Portland twenty days after his twentieth birthday.

"I think he could go out and play for a triple-double every night and get it," teammate Jeff McInnis said. "But he doesn't play for that, and that's a credit to him."[3] More and more, James's dominant games would lead to Cleveland victories. "[W]e're winning," he said. "And I'm happy."[4]

In 2004–05, James became just the second Cavalier ever to start in the NBA All-Star Game. He totaled 13 points, 8 rebounds, and 6 assists in the contest. He went on to set several franchise records, including a new scoring mark of 27.2 points per game. James became the youngest player in history named to a postseason All-NBA Team (a second-team honor). He also was the fifth player ever to average at least 27 points, 7 rebounds, and 7 assists per game.

New Bosses, New Heights

On June 2, 2005, the Cavaliers named Mike Brown their seventeenth head coach. The Cavaliers would have to admit fate was smiling on them. The thirty-five-year-old Brown had been Indiana's associate head coach the previous two seasons. Pacers head coach Rick Carlisle pointed to his past tutoring of elite players as a keen indicator of his potential in Cleveland. "There is no one more ready to become a first-time head coach in the NBA than Mike Brown," Carlisle noted. "His experience working with MVP-caliber players like Jermaine O'Neal and Tim Duncan has prepared him well to help LeBron James continue to develop into one of

There is an old saying that it is good to be the king, and LeBron James would be hard-pressed to argue as he gives a hello kiss to pop diva Beyonce Knowles.

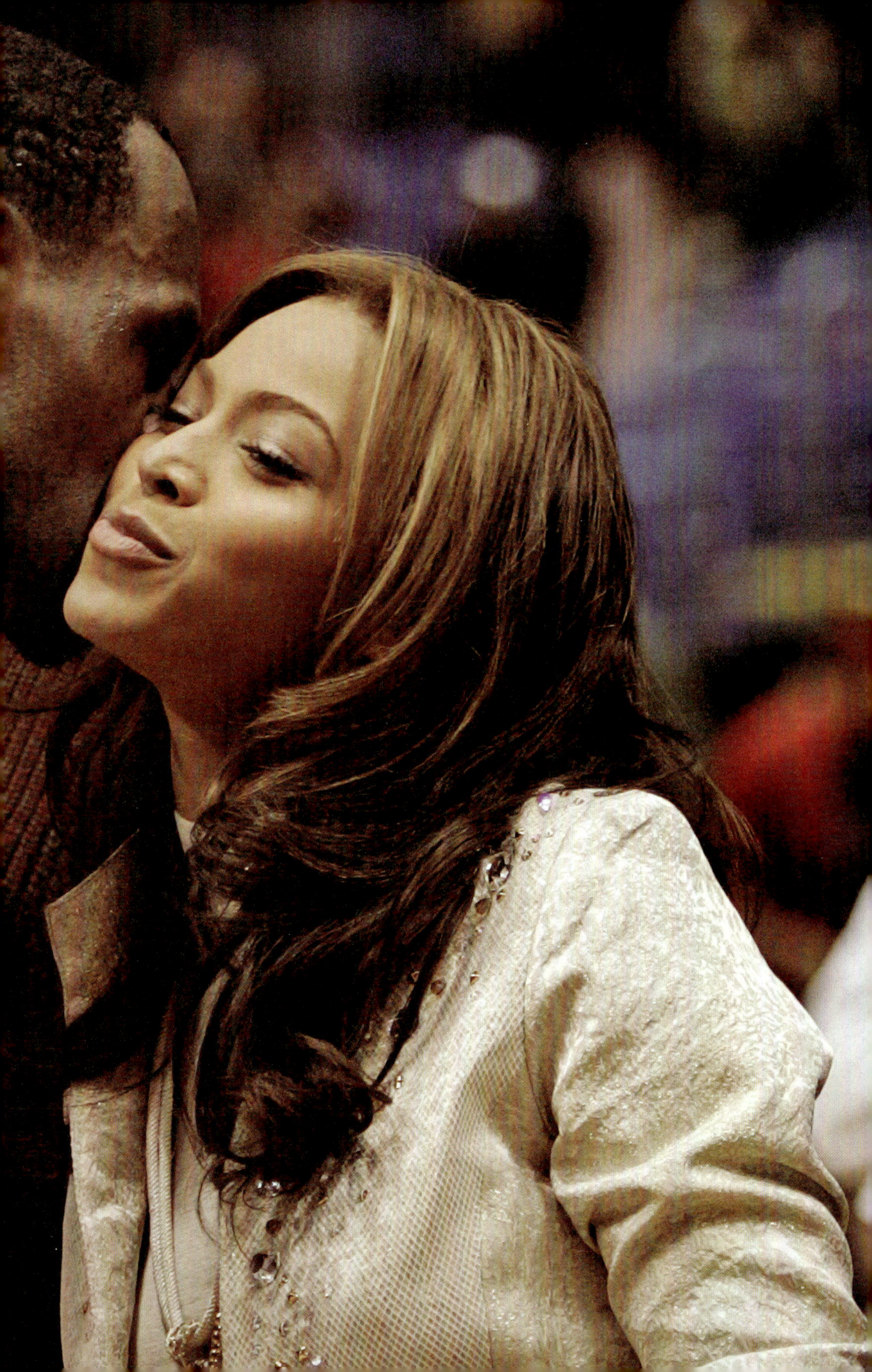

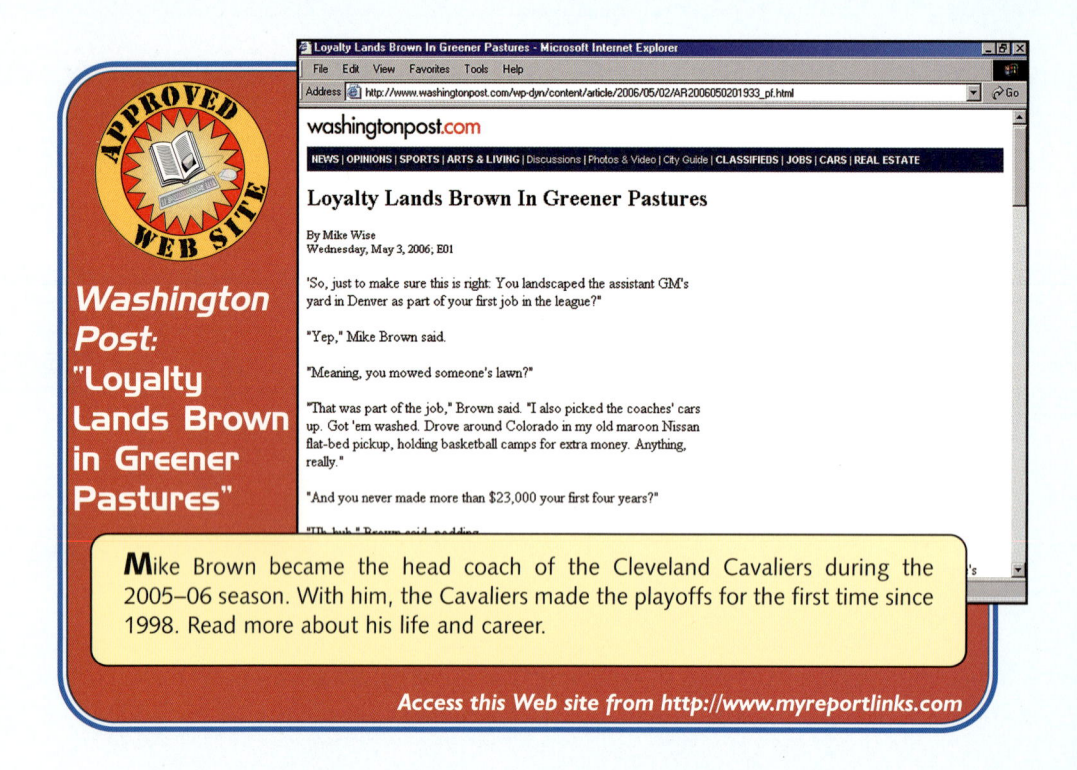

Washington Post: "Loyalty Lands Brown in Greener Pastures"

> Mike Brown became the head coach of the Cleveland Cavaliers during the 2005–06 season. With him, the Cavaliers made the playoffs for the first time since 1998. Read more about his life and career.

Access this Web site from http://www.myreportlinks.com

the all-time greats. This is a slam-dunk hire for the Cleveland Cavaliers."[5]

Brown called James shortly after accepting the job and suggested a meeting between the two. Recalled Brown: "I asked him, 'LeBron, what do you like to do? Do you like to bowl or would you like to go to dinner? I'd like to get together real soon.' He said, 'Coach, I'm going to an amusement park real soon, do you want to come?' I forget he's a kid."[6]

Later that month, majority owner Dan Gilbert rounded out his staff. He hired former Cavaliers player Danny Ferry to serve as general manager at the age of thirty-eight. Ferry had spent the two previous seasons as San Antonio's director of basketball operations, winning a 2005 NBA championship ring. Somehow, it seemed fitting that a pair of thirty-somethings would now be steering a team led by one of the youngest NBA superstars in history.

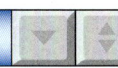

A Season of Streaks

Brown won his first game as head coach, as James scored 31 points in a 109–87 rout of the New Orleans Hornets. The Cavaliers then dropped two straight, but next reeled off eight consecutive wins to jump squarely among the NBA's teams to watch. More excitement followed during a season that was, in many ways, built on surges. The Cavaliers enjoyed separate strings of nine, eight, seven, and six wins in a row in 2005–06. They also suffered slumps of five and six straight games, but the good outweighed the bad. Cleveland won 50 games (50–32) for the first time since 1992–93. The Cavs finished second in the Central Division and returned to the playoffs after an eight-year absence.

It was not just James, either, though he ranked third in the NBA in scoring average (31.4) and second in minutes (42.5). Center Zydrunas Ilgauskas contributed more than 15 points per game while combining with Drew Gooden to help the Cavs amass a big rebounding advantage over

Former Cavaliers player Danny Ferry was hired by the Cavs in 2005 to be the team's general manager. Head coach Mike Brown is standing next to him on the left.

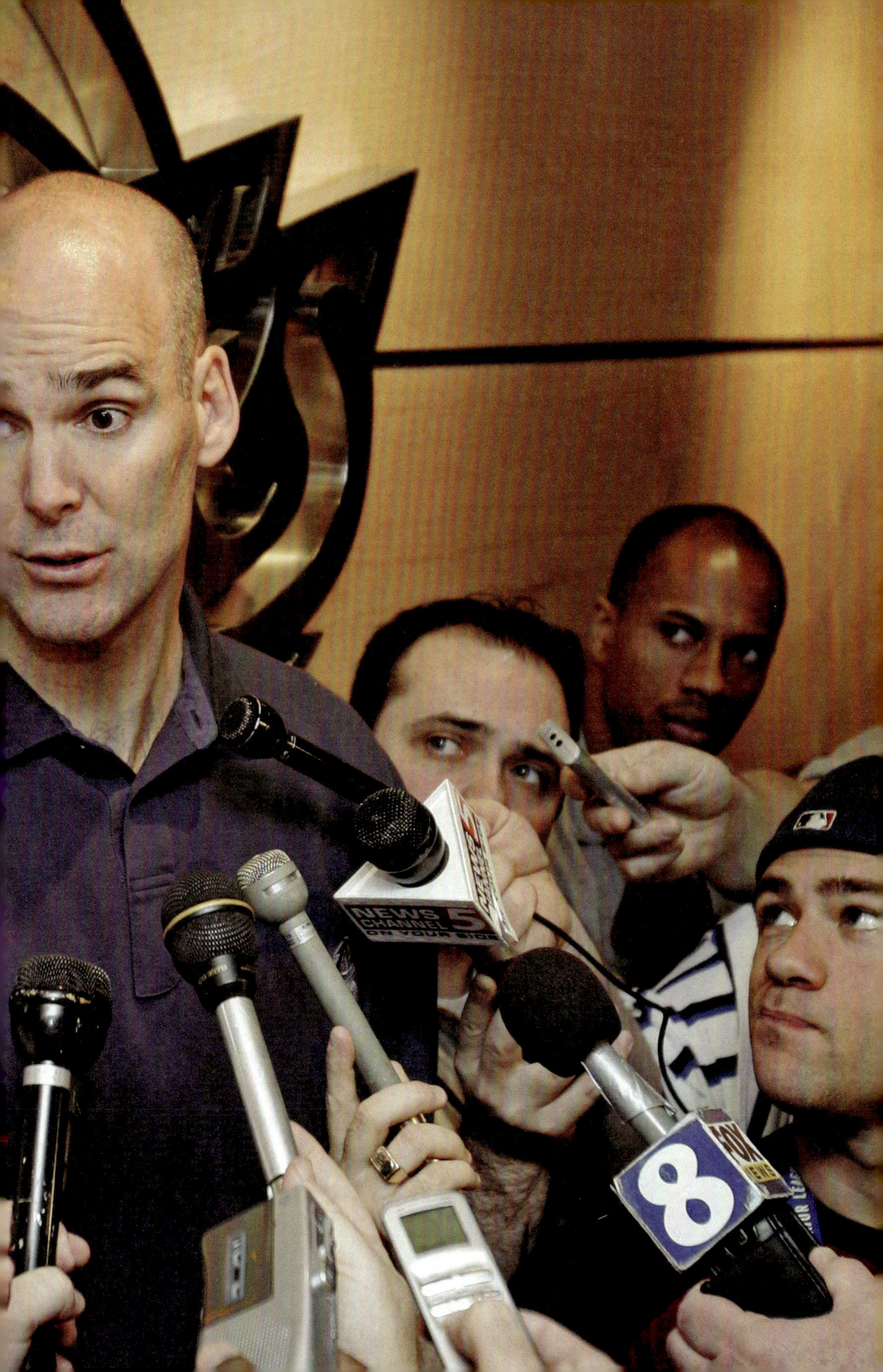
NEWS CHANNEL 5
ON YOUR SIDE
8
FOX NEWS

their opponents. Moreover, Donyell Marshall was a great spark plug off the bench.

In the middle of it all was a memorable All-Star Game performance by James. Some called it his coming-out party. His East team trailed by seventeen points at halftime, but James erupted for 13 points in the first six minutes of the third quarter, thanks in part to back-to-back three-pointers. James finished with 29, and his block of Tracy McGrady's potential game-tying jumper secured a 122–120 East victory. He was voted the All-Star Game's MVP.

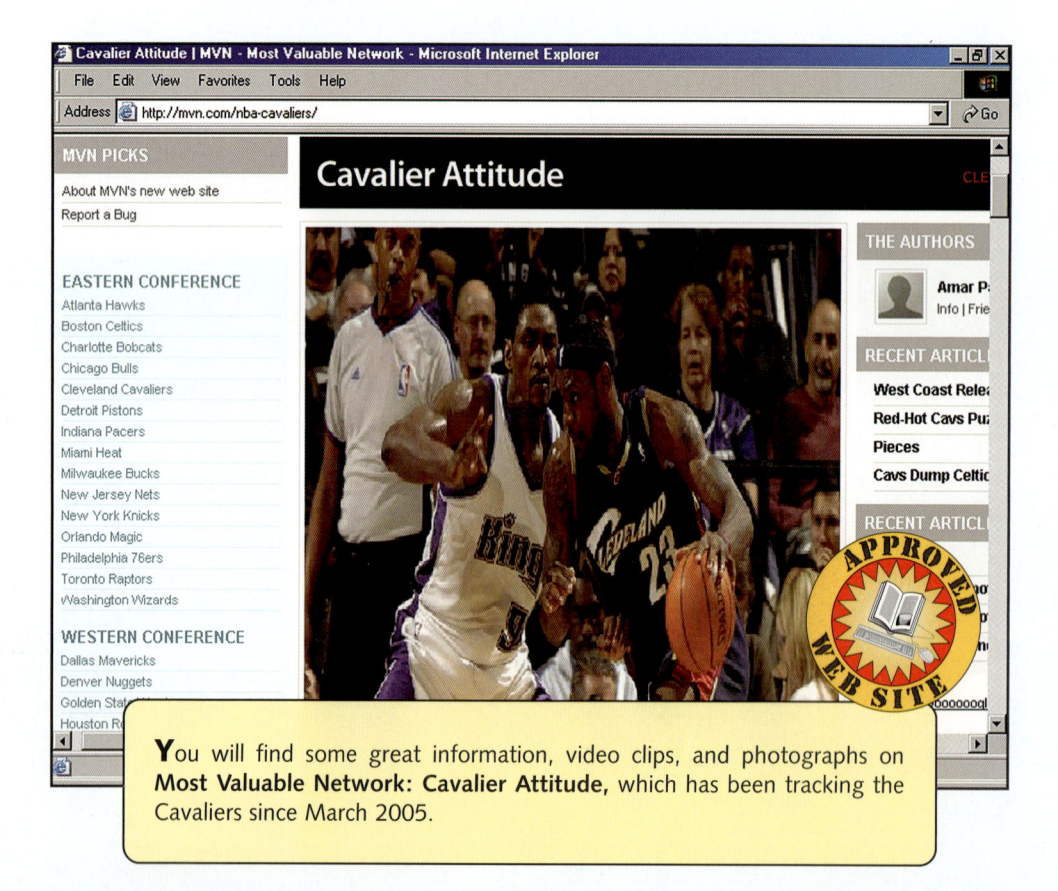

You will find some great information, video clips, and photographs on **Most Valuable Network: Cavalier Attitude,** which has been tracking the Cavaliers since March 2005.

Drew Gooden skies for a rebound in this November 2006 contest against the Memphis Grizzlies. The Cavs traded for Gooden prior to the 2004–05 season.

MyReportLinks.com Books

ESPN.com: The Playoffs

In 2007, the Cleveland Cavaliers reached the NBA Finals for the first time in team history. On this ESPN Web site you can read about this four-game series. Game recaps, video footage, interviews, photos, and more can be found here.

Access this Web site from http://www.myreportlinks.com

April 1, no fooling, might have been an even more memorable day for "King James" and the Cavaliers. Facing the Miami Heat and fellow highlight-reel performer Dwyane Wade, James put on a show like few had ever seen. He and Wade matched dazzling shots and dunks over much of the night. When it was over, James was on top. His 47 points, 12 rebounds, and 10 assists pushed Cleveland to a 106–99 victory. Wade's 44 points, 9 assists, and 8 rebounds, believe it or not, were not enough. "People got a view of absolute greatness," Miami coach Pat Riley described. "It's absolutely beyond description."[7]

By season's end, Cleveland fans had taken to chanting "M-V-P! M-V-P!" when James had the ball. They proved to be nearly prophetic. James finished second to Steve Nash in the voting for the NBA MVP Award—an extraordinary accomplishment for a twenty-one year old.

Putting the "Play" in Playoffs

Playoff disappointment has been synonymous with the Cavaliers. Ten of their first thirteen trips to the postseason ended in first-round defeat. Of course, James was not even born for many of the first-round Cleveland exits, and he was too young to remember or put much stock in the rest. He made sure his own playoff career got off to a winning—some might even say legendary—start.

In Game 1 of the 2006 Eastern Conference quarterfinals, James amassed 32 points, 11 rebounds, and 11 assists. The performance gave the fourth-seeded Cavs a 97–86 home triumph over fifth-seeded Washington. James became the first player since Magic Johnson to notch a triple-double in his postseason debut. "He never ceases to amaze me," Brown noted. "The things that he does offensively just blow you away. He does it in the flow of the game, which is what makes him special."[8]

More magic followed. With the series tied 2–2, James's dramatic bucket with less than a second to play in overtime gave the Cavaliers a 121–120 triumph in Game 5. Two nights later, his 32 points clinched a deciding victory over the Wizards and the Cavs' first playoff series win since 1993.

The Cavaliers nearly extended their season against the powerful Detroit Pistons in the Eastern Conference semifinals. James recorded a second triple-double as Cleveland won three straight after dropping the first two games on the road. However, Detroit rebounded to claim the final two games and the series. James and the Cavaliers had come oh-so-close to upsetting the heavily favored Pistons.

Among the Elite

The Cavaliers entered the 2006–07 season ranked as the seventh best team in the NBA, according to *USA Today*. Explosive guard Larry Hughes, who missed most of the previous season due to injury, took much of the scoring burden off James. Meanwhile, big men Zydrunas Ilgauskas and Drew Gooden were each capable of producing a double-double on any night. Guard Eric Snow rounded out the starting five, bringing leadership and aggressive defense to the lineup.

The Cavs surged after the All-Star break in 2006–07, as James threw his game into high gear. In one contest against Milwaukee, he scored 16 points in the fourth quarter and set up the

The King James Era

FIRST FOUR YEARS IN THE NBA

PLAYER	G	GS	REB	RPG	AST	APG	STL	BLK	PTS	PPG
LeBron James	316	316	2,102	6.7	2,033	6.4	555	231	8,439	26.7
Kobe Bryant	266	119	1,054	4.0	803	3.0	301	175	4,240	15.9
Kevin Garnett	286	249	2,394	8.4	931	3.3	408	527	4,639	16.2
Tracy McGrady	269	130	1,628	6.1	826	3.1	307	396	4,187	15.6
Jermaine O'Neal	211	18	651	3.1	56	0.3	32	153	817	3.9

G=Games played GS=Games started REB=Rebounds RPG=Rebounds per game
AST=Assists APG=Assists per game STL=Steals BLK=Blocks
PTS=Points scored PPG=Points per game

▲ LeBron James went straight from high school to the NBA. Here is how his first four years in the league compared to the first four seasons of four other NBA stars that made the jump from high school to the pros.

winning shot in the final seconds. In a game at Detroit—where Cleveland had struggled for years—he burned the Pistons for 41 points in a Cavaliers victory. The Cavs finished 50–32, storming into the playoffs. In Round 1, Cleveland swept the Washington Wizards in four games. New Jersey fell to the Cavs in five games in the second round. Then, the Cavaliers defeated the Pistons 98–82 in Game 6 of the Eastern Conference Finals. That win gave the Cleveland franchise its first NBA Finals appearance.

The Cavs opponent in the finals was the ultra-tough San Antonio Spurs, a team with a stingy defense. Led by Tony Parker and Tim Duncan, the Spurs frustrated James and the Cavs. San Antonio swept the series in four games. Although the Cavs were eliminated, they now knew what it took to become NBA champs.

Bill Fitch was the first head coach in Cleveland Cavaliers history.

CAVS IN CHARGE

The Cleveland Cavaliers cannot be accused of not giving stability a chance. Despite their struggling ways as an NBA expansion team, they gave initial head coach Bill Fitch nine seasons to try to build a champion. Since then, change has been the norm. Through it all, some of the club's coaches and general managers have stood out. Those men are featured below, as is the legendary voice that continues to carry the Cavaliers' exploits to the ears of their fans.

Bill Fitch

If ever a man seemed built to handle the trials and tribulations of coaching a poorly stocked NBA expansion team, it was Bill Fitch. Throughout his coaching career, Fitch was a man many teams would bring aboard to turn around their ailing franchises. One reason he seemed such a perfect fit for Cleveland—his first NBA head coaching stop—was his unfailing sense of humor. "We were the only team in history that could lose nine straight games and then go into a slump," Fitch once said.[1]

And lose they did. The Cavs dropped fifteen consecutive games to begin Fitch's pro career. Before one game during the slump, Fitch was stopped by a security guard as he tried to enter an arena. Instead of reaching for his identification, the coach matter-of-factly asked if the security guard knew anyone else who would admit to coaching the Cavaliers. The guard, no doubt laughing, let Fitch walk in.

Coach of the Year

His team also suffered from an identity crisis. Fitch once said it would stump the panel of the hit TV show *What's My Line?* And of adding the six-foot eleven-inch Walt Wesley and six-foot ten-inch Luke Rackley off other teams' scrap heaps in the expansion draft, he quipped, "At least we have two players who can almost look Kareem Abdul-Jabbar in the eye."[2]

Fitch turned out to be much more than a laugh-a-minute for the Cavaliers and their fans. He endured that awful 15–67 first season. He gradually worked in better talent and improved the Cavs' win totals in each of the next two years. He guided the club to 40 wins in its fifth season, putting it on the brink of becoming a playoff club. And in 1975–76, he became the first—and through 2006, the only—Cavalier to be honored as NBA Coach of the Year.

Fitch did it the only way he knew how. He stressed teamwork. The Cavaliers might not have suited up the biggest stars of the day. But together, Fitch stressed, they could be world-beaters. Putting one of the NBA's deepest teams on the floor, and a group that got along off the court as well as it did on it, Fitch coaxed the club to a 49–33 record and the Central Division title in

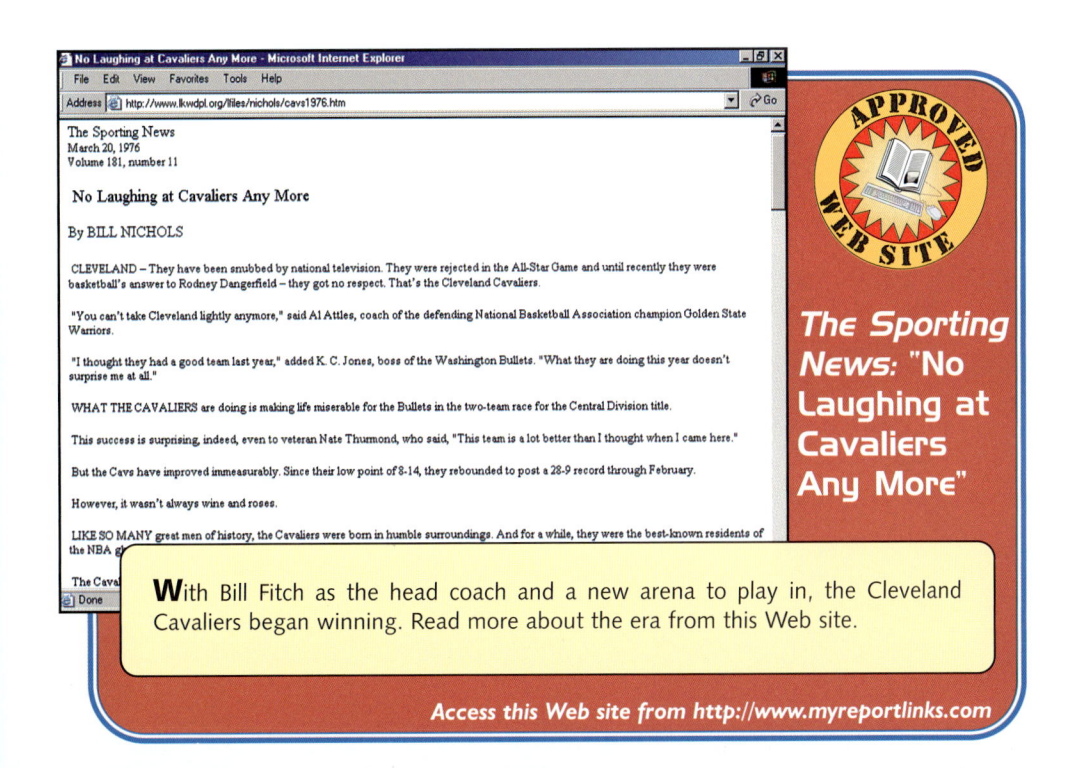

The Sporting News: "No Laughing at Cavaliers Any More"

With Bill Fitch as the head coach and a new arena to play in, the Cleveland Cavaliers began winning. Read more about the era from this Web site.

Access this Web site from http://www.myreportlinks.com

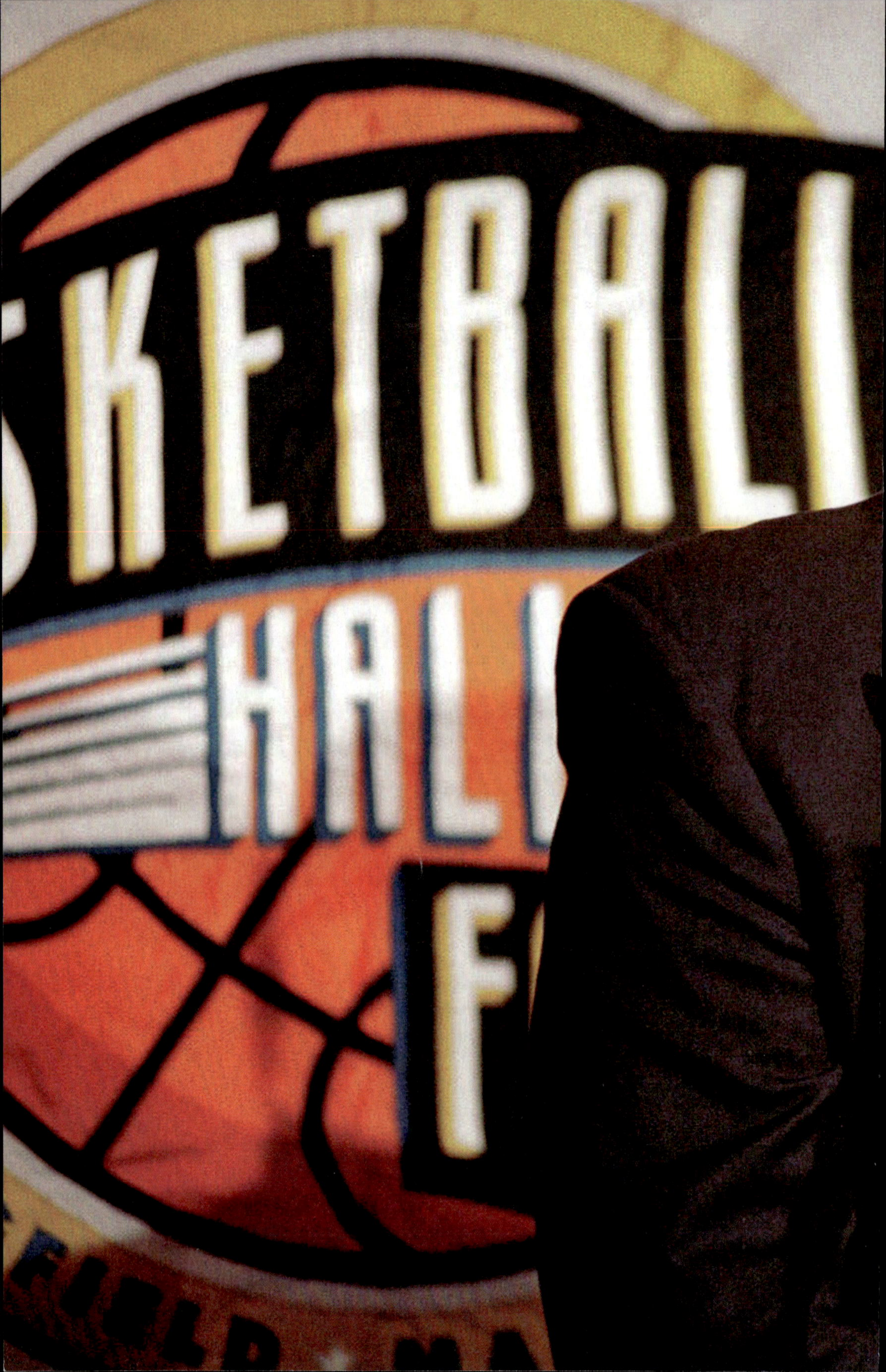

Wayne Embry blazed a new trail when he became the first African-American general manager of an NBA franchise. Embry's name is enshrined in the Naismith Memorial Basketball Hall of Fame.

1975–76. An article in *The Sporting News* declared that Fitch did it with "patience, some glue, baling wire and frugal use of Eagle Stamps."[3]

That was the pinnacle of Fitch's Cleveland tenure. The Cavaliers' 1978–79 slide marked the end of the first coaching era in franchise history, but it did not mark the end of Fitch. The Cavs' favorite funny man became the head coach of the Celtics, whom he led to an NBA championship in 1981. Fitch later coached the Rockets, Nets, and Clippers over a twenty-five-year head coaching career. In 1997, he was named one of the top ten coaches in NBA history.

Wayne Embry

Wayne Embry was already a trailblazer by the time the Cavaliers hired him to serve as vice president and general manager in 1986. The Milwaukee Bucks had made the former NBA big man the league's first African-American general manager nearly fifteen years earlier. "[H]e was a pioneer," noted author Richard Lapchick. "Like all pioneers, he faced hard times and incredible challenges. Ultimately, Wayne Embry's life is an inspiration to everyone who has been told that they cannot get to the top."[4]

Embry's tenure at the Cavaliers helm was a homecoming. He had grown up in Springfield, Ohio, led Miami University of Ohio in scoring, and was a five-time all-star with the NBA's Cincinnati Royals. Embry's arrival in Cleveland coincided with the best draft in club history. Over an eleven-year stretch, the Cavs posted ten winning seasons.

Embry was not finished breaking barriers, either. Known as "The Wall" during his playing days for his willingness to set hard picks, he kept knocking walls down during his front-office career. In 1994, he became the first African-American team president and chief operating officer in NBA history—roles he held until leaving the team in 2000.

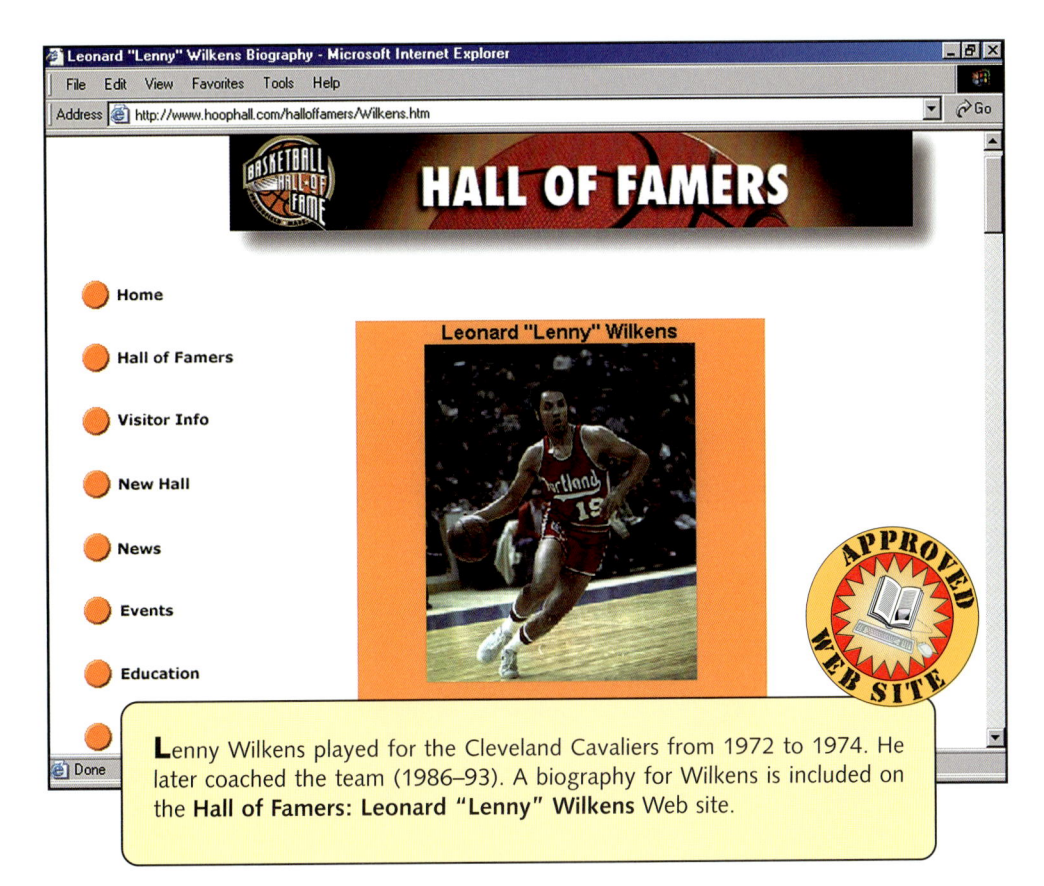

Lenny Wilkens played for the Cleveland Cavaliers from 1972 to 1974. He later coached the team (1986–93). A biography for Wilkens is included on the **Hall of Famers: Leonard "Lenny" Wilkens** Web site.

Embry endured his share of bad press along the way. Some fans in Milwaukee still remember him as the man who traded Kareem Abdul-Jabbar to the Lakers. And his Cleveland clubs made it as far as the Eastern Conference Finals just once. Still, his impact in his home state and on the Cavaliers is impossible to deny. *The Sporting News* named Embry NBA Executive of the Year in 1992 and 1998, and *Sports Illustrated* also gave him that same honor in 1998. In 1999, Embry was inducted into the Basketball Hall of Fame.

Lenny Wilkens

Having a point guard like Wilkens running the offense was like having an extra coach on the floor. Thus, it came as little surprise to those who knew him as a poised and cerebral floor general that he went on to become the winningest coach in NBA history, surpassing Boston Celtics legend Red Auerbach. By the time Wilkens took Cleveland's head coaching job in 1986, he had already accomplished more than most bench bosses manage in a lifetime. In 1977–78, he took over a 5–17 Seattle club and guided it to that season's NBA Finals. The next year, he led the Sonics to the NBA championship.

His turnaround of the Cavaliers' fortunes was not quite that dramatic, but it was no small chore, either. George Karl and Gene Littles had combined

Mike Fratello's fiery attitude sparked the Cavaliers when he took over as head coach in 1993. He coached the team until the end of the 1998–99 season.

to win just 29 games the previous season. The main problem was defense. In his first season, Wilkens's Cavs limited foes to two fewer points per game, and the modest result was two more wins. Then the fun began.

In 1987–88, with Brad Daugherty and Mark Price leading the way, the Cavaliers surged to the playoffs with their best record in ten years. And in 1988–89, Wilkens found himself coaching the Eastern Conference All-Stars en route to a 57–25 mark, the best in team history.

"I've always believed you need balance," Wilkens once told the *Boston Globe* about his coaching philosophy. "[E]ven if you have a star, it's important to surround him with the right kind of complementary players."[5]

Wilkens followed that formula to great success in Cleveland. He enjoyed three 50-win seasons in his seven-year tenure and led the team to its second conference finals appearance in 1992. During his Cavaliers coaching run, Wilkens was inducted into the Basketball Hall of Fame as a player in 1989. Nine years later, he became one of three men enshrined as both a player and a coach.

Mike Fratello

As successful as Wilkens was in the victory column, there is one thing he was not for the Cavaliers—a madman. And at least one Cavs player felt that was precisely what the club needed following a sweep at the hands of the Bulls in the second round of the 1993 playoffs. "Changes are coming," Gerald Wilkins told *The Sporting News* after the loss. "You can feel it. Maybe we need someone to come in (as coach) who is a little bit of a madman. Someone who will make us do one-handed push-ups and run through brick walls for him. Maybe that's exactly what we need."[6]

Five days later, Wilkens announced his resignation as head coach. And a month after that, former Atlanta Hawks coach Mike Fratello was named

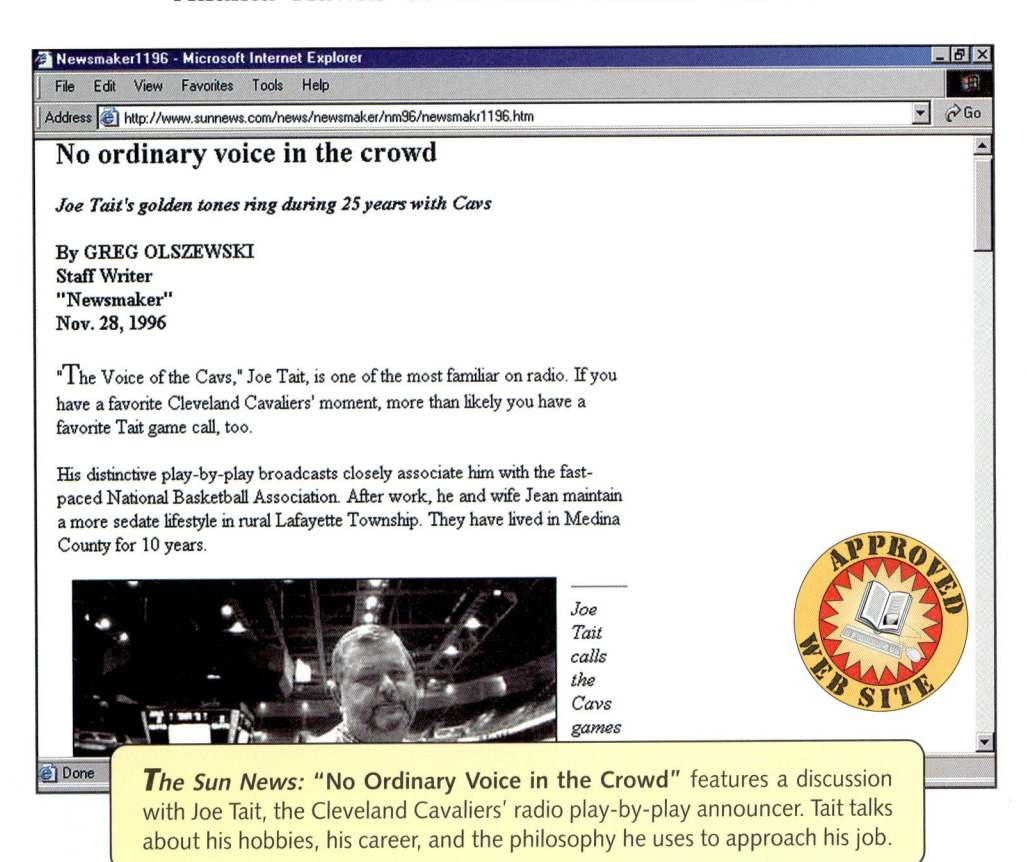

No ordinary voice in the crowd

Joe Tait's golden tones ring during 25 years with Cavs

By GREG OLSZEWSKI
Staff Writer
"Newsmaker"
Nov. 28, 1996

"The Voice of the Cavs," Joe Tait, is one of the most familiar on radio. If you have a favorite Cleveland Cavaliers' moment, more than likely you have a favorite Tait game call, too.

His distinctive play-by-play broadcasts closely associate him with the fast-paced National Basketball Association. After work, he and wife Jean maintain a more sedate lifestyle in rural Lafayette Township. They have lived in Medina County for 10 years.

Joe Tait calls the Cavs games

The Sun News: "No Ordinary Voice in the Crowd" features a discussion with Joe Tait, the Cleveland Cavaliers' radio play-by-play announcer. Tait talks about his hobbies, his career, and the philosophy he uses to approach his job.

his replacement. Fratello was not known as a madman, per sé. But the driven nature of the son of a New Jersey boxer was well established. "There's . . . [a] kind of passion for winning," Cavaliers GM Wayne Embry said of his new coach. "That's what competition is all about."[7]

➲ Coach and Broadcaster

Play-by-play man Marv Albert had nicknamed Fratello "Czar of the Telestrator" for his ability to diagram plays for television viewers as an NBC analyst. That followed a seven-year run as Hawks coach in which Fratello posted four straight 50-win seasons and was named 1986 Coach of the Year. His return to the bench with the Cavaliers looked to be a perfect fit for a talented team in need of a championship-caliber spark.

Fratello clashed often with his players as the Cavaliers moved from a methodical, half-court approach to a quicker pace. They won 47, 43, and 47 games in Fratello's first three seasons, but they bowed out in the first round of the playoffs every time. They missed the playoffs in 1996–97 but returned the following season with another 47–35 mark—only to be sent home early again.

Finally, after enduring his first two losing campaigns with the club, Fratello resumed his broadcasting career. His players might not have run through walls or fulfilled their championship dreams, but his 248 Cleveland wins ranked third on the franchise's career list.

Joe Tait

Only one man in Cavaliers history has had his belly immortalized. Play-by-play man Joe Tait might tell you that is not necessarily a high honor.

It is Tait's delightful voice, not his midsection, that has made him a legend in northeast Ohio. But in 2002, the Cavaliers gave out five thousand Joe Tait Bobble-belly dolls to commemorate his 2,500th game. Tait, to no one's surprise, turned the promotion into material for the comedy routines that often accompany his broadcasts.

Washington Post: "Ferry Rises From Front Row to the Cavaliers' Front Office"

Danny Ferry was named general manager of the Cleveland Cavaliers in 2005. He had previously played on with the team for the better part of a decade. Learn more about his life on this Web site.

Access this Web site from http://www.myreportlinks.com

Quips are a way of life for Tait, and why not? He has been with the Cavaliers since their inception, having been hired to call their very first game in 1970. "Remember, I also did the Cleveland Indians for years," Tait once said, referring to a fourteen-year stretch of broadcasting Cleveland baseball during the summer. "I have probably seen more losses than any other human being on the planet."[8]

Tait has won over listeners with his flowing delivery, knowledge of basketball, and ability to interject opinion without coming off as a shameless "homer." He has won numerous Sportscaster of the Year awards and is a member of several halls of fame.

➔ Danny Ferry

The son of an NBA general manager, Danny Ferry has never been far from the game. As a child, he rebounded missed shots for the likes of Washington Bullets stars Wes Unseld and Mitch Kupchak. He also accompanied his father to dinners with such masterminds as legendary Celtics coach Red Auerbach.

So it was not a stretch when Cleveland, looking for a general manager before the 2005–06 season, turned to the former Duke University National Player of the Year. Ferry was thirty-eight at the time, taking the reins as the youngest GM in the league. He had spent thirteen years as a player for the Cavaliers and Spurs, winning an NBA championship with San Antonio in 2003. He added a second title in 2005, his second year as the Spurs' director of basketball operations.

That is another thing about Ferry. Wherever he goes, success seems to follow. The Spurs were reluctant to see him go. "We haven't found anybody for his slot," Spurs coach Gregg Popovich told *The Washington Post* early in the 2005–06 season. Popovich noted that Ferry's replacement had not yet been named "because we haven't found his equal."[9]

If Ferry's first two seasons as GM are any indication of things to come, the Cavaliers could be on their way to great success. They made the playoffs for the first time in nine years, reached the NBA Finals for the first time ever, and served notice that the best is yet to come.

The deciding game of the 2006 Eastern Conference semifinals between the Cleveland Cavaliers and Detroit Pistons was played on Detroit's home court. Yet these Cavs fans came out to the Quicken Loans Arena just to watch the game on the big screen.

GAME DAY

Cleveland rocks! Especially during the NBA playoffs. In "Loudville," fans can cheer the Cavaliers for the same price as a hot dog and soft drink at other NBA arenas. "This is where the real fans are," said Michael DiFilippo from his top-row seat at Quicken Loans Arena during the 2006 Eastern Conference semifinals.[1]

The upper reaches of the building have come to be known as "Loudville" for the amount of noise produced. Postseason tickets there could be purchased for as little as fourteen dollars. "They may not hear me individually," added fan Darryl Lewis, "but us collectively as a group? We're gonna make a difference."[2]

Distinctively Cleveland

One of the many beauties of Quicken Loans Arena—or "The Q," as Clevelanders call it—is that those "Loudville" seats offer a terrific view of the game. When you hear "there's not a bad seat in the house," it is completely accurate in Cleveland. The Q's architects made sure of that.

"Loudville" circles the top of the arena and offers the most affordable view of a Cavaliers game. But about 60 percent of the twenty-thousand-plus seats are located in the lower bowl of the downtown arena. The blue seats all point toward center court.

The Q and Downtown Cleveland

The prices of professional sports tickets have skyrocketed everywhere in recent years. Cleveland is no exception. However, attending a Cavaliers game does not have to break the bank. Sure, you can pay top dollar and lounge in the Mercedes-Benz Club area, where gourmet food will make your game night a five-star experience. But during 2005–06, a fan could watch the Cavaliers make the playoffs for the first time in nine years for a mere ten dollars during the regular season. Regular-season seats in the center of the upper level ranged between thirty-five and fifty dollars.

The Q, then known as Gund Arena, opened in 1994 as part of the Historic Gateway Neighborhood project to revitalize a large area of downtown Cleveland. The Gateway Sports and Entertainment Complex includes Jacobs Field, where baseball's Cleveland Indians play. The complex also features one of the best collections of public art in the country.

➲ "Uniquely Cleveland"

The Cavaliers had previously played at suburban Richfield Coliseum. The opening of their state-of-the-art downtown home provided a window—quite literally—to the richness of Cleveland's heritage. The Q's most distinctive feature is its 108-foot by 48-foot bay window that allows those on the outside to see in. From the inside, patrons are treated to a sensational view of the Cleveland Industrial Flats. The

Quicken Loans Arena - Microsoft Internet Explorer

Address: http://basketball.ballparks.com/NBA/ClevelandCavaliers/index.htm

Ticket Dogs
These Dogs Can Hunt... For Your Tickets

The Quicken Loans Arena

APPROVED WEB SITE

This latest home of the Cleveland Cavaliers was completed in 1994. State of the art technology was installed in the complex and includes ArenaVision and Fanimation boards. Read more about the amenities when you visit this **Quicken Loans Arena** Web page.

magnificent window is one of several touches that gives the arena a "uniquely Cleveland" appeal.

Amenities at the Q

The Quicken Loans Arena features a top-of-the-line sound system. The four-sided ArenaVision gives fans instant replay and up-to-the-minute statistics. The Q also boasts four full-color "Fanimation" boards hung in the corners of the building. These provide scores, stats, and in-game messages.

At last count, the arena included 562 television monitors. Hungry and thirsty fans do not have to miss one moment of the action when visiting the plentiful concession areas. Many of those in the food lines salivate for Quaker Steak & Lube chicken wings. The famed restaurant that originated in nearby western Pennsylvania has two locations inside The Q. One is in Gordon's Sports Bar, a full-service restaurant on the main concourse.

For a delicious Cleveland favorite, fans swarm to Panini's in Section 125. The restaurant's popular, overstuffed sandwich is piled high with grilled deli meat, cheese, coleslaw, and tomatoes on French bread, and it comes with fresh-cut fries. One of these should hold you over until the fourth quarter, when a stop at one of the arena's soft-serve ice cream or Dippin' Dots stands might be in order.

Game Day

➲ Game Night Fun

Joe Tait, radio voice of the Cavaliers, starts every home game with the call, "It's basketball time at Quicken Loans Arena!" But "basketball time" means much more than just a game at an NBA arena nowadays, and The Q is no exception. Cavaliers staffers put on a show from the moment the fans walk through the doors.

The game night emcee is Canadian-born sports personality Olivier Sedra, who began handling the Cavs' public-address announcing during the

Find the latest news from around the league on **NBA.com,** the official Web site of the NBA. You will be able to learn about the league's history, teams, players, and more.

EDITOR'S CHOICE

2006–07 season. His enthusiasm might be a little over the top at times; nevertheless, Sedra injects boundless energy into each and every game.

Moondog

Then there is Moondog, the popular mascot who does the same thing without saying a word. He is not the most obedient canine, which can be a problem when he stands six feet tall on hind legs and weighs 200 pounds. But he is housebroken, and Moondog keeps fans howling with his hilarious antics in the stands and on the court during breaks in the action.

If you are wondering how the Cavaliers wound up with a pooch for a mascot, consider Cleveland's musical history. Legendary Cleveland radio deejay Alan Freed was credited with popularizing the phrase "rock and roll" in the 1950s. This claim to fame played no small role in the Rock and Roll Hall of Fame's location near the shores of Lake Erie. Freed's nickname was Moondog.

The oversized, furry Moondog that roams the Quicken Loans Arena aisles has some serious hops. He won the 2004 Mascot Madness competition by showcasing a variety of dunks and trick shots. Moondog once routed Boston Celtics star Paul Pierce in an impromptu half-court shooting contest. On one occasion, he was fined by the NBA for excessively "hounding" an opposing player.

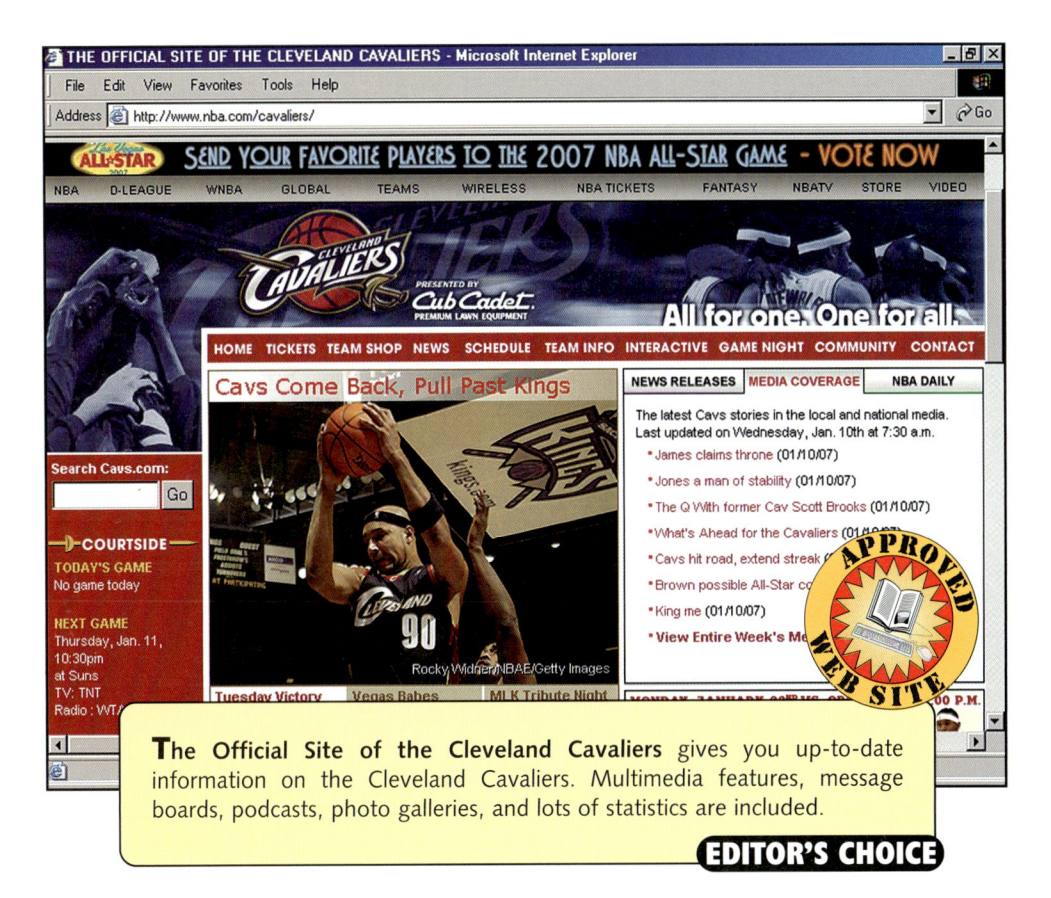

Game Day

The Official Site of the Cleveland Cavaliers gives you up-to-date information on the Cleveland Cavaliers. Multimedia features, message boards, podcasts, photo galleries, and lots of statistics are included.

EDITOR'S CHOICE

Needless to say, the Cleveland fans had no problem with their puppy's behavior.

Moondog does require an "Animal Control" unit. This group of chaperones in blue jumpsuits keeps the mascot from spending the entire game in the vicinity of the Cavalier Girls or the Scream Team. The Cavalier Girls' dance routines would never have you guessing that their "day jobs" range from seamstresses to law students.

The Scream Team's performances include not only traditional dancing, but also tumbling and break dancing. "King Headspin" is the star of the latter. And a night of basketball in northeast Ohio might not be complete without an appearance by "Beefcake on the Lake." They are billed as "the biggest dance team in Ohio . . . literally." This group of a dozen shakin' big fellas has to be seen to be believed.

Following the Cavs

If you cannot make it to a live game, you can still follow the Cavs up close. The radio and TV personalities who broadcast their games are some of the best in the business. As the 2006–07 season got under way, Joe Tait celebrated his thirty-fifth season as the radio voice of the Cavaliers. Mike Snyder entered his fifteenth consecutive year as Tait's informative and reliable studio host.

Television play-by-play man Frank McLeod has more than two decades broadcasting experience on his résumé. A pair of former Cleveland Cavs players—Austin Carr and Scott Williams—contribute insightful color commentary on the local networks that carry the games. The 2005–06 season marked the second consecutive year that all eighty-two regular-season Cavaliers games were televised. Broadcast ratings have soared since the arrival of LeBron James in 2003–04.

Sports Business Journal in 2005 ranked the Cavaliers official Web site the No. 1 site in the NBA and No. 10 in all of professional sports. That

Game Day

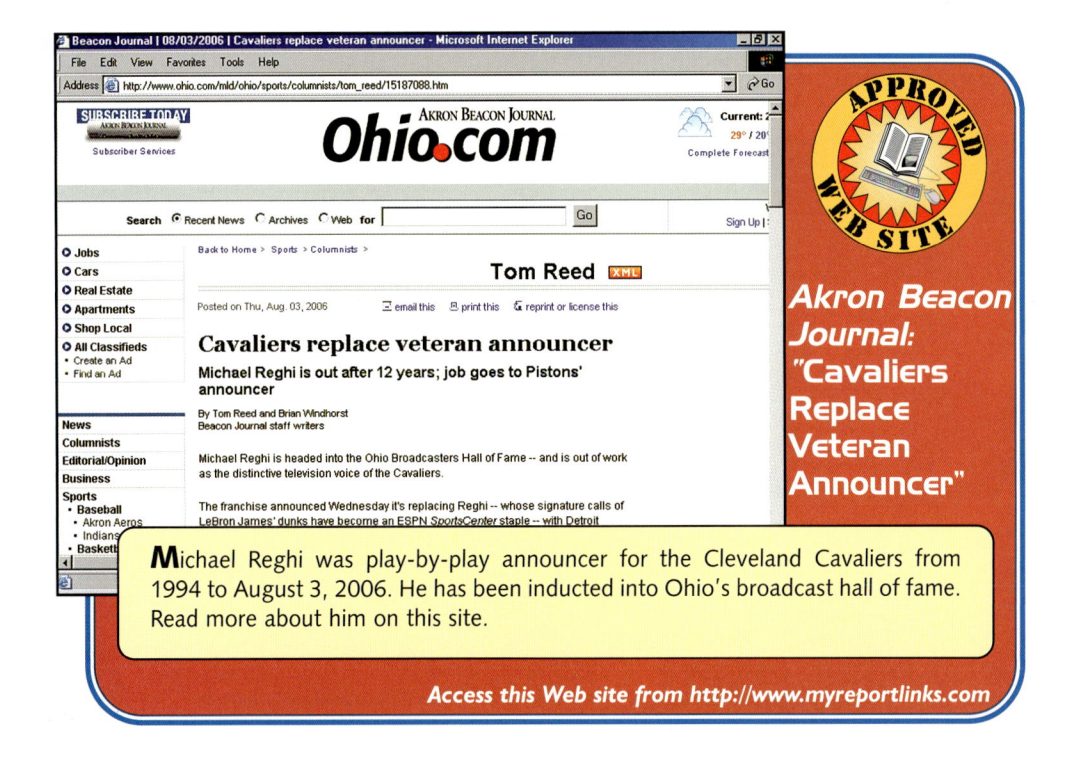

Akron Beacon Journal: "Cavaliers Replace Veteran Announcer"

Michael Reghi was play-by-play announcer for the Cleveland Cavaliers from 1994 to August 3, 2006. He has been inducted into Ohio's broadcast hall of fame. Read more about him on this site.

Access this Web site from http://www.myreportlinks.com

was also the year the site underwent a major redesign, which produced a more fan-friendly Web experience.

"The leading source for information about the team, Cavs dot-com has taken on a life of its own," Cavaliers President Len Komoroski noted. "Fans want a connection to the team and to the players. The new Cavs dot-com provides that connection in an exciting multi-faceted, multi-media format."[3]

In addition to providing the latest statistics, schedules, and game information, Cavs dot-com also features its own beat writer/columnist. Joe Gabriele is nicknamed "The Optimist" and makes no bones about his love of the home team.

Former Cavaliers player World B. Free acknowledges the crowd as he is honored by the team in 2005.

THE HEROES 7

Imagine Mark Price bringing the ball upcourt and using his remarkable vision to free up LeBron James for easy shots. How about James drawing a double-team on the perimeter and bouncing a pass inside to Brad Daugherty? Or James connecting with the high-flying Larry Nance on an alley-oop? A championship has yet to come the Cavaliers' way, but their loyal fans have been treated to a unique blend of personalities and superstars over the last three and a half decades.

➲ Bingo Smith

For early fans of the Cavaliers, several things about Bobby Smith made the small forward unforgettable. Foremost was his nickname, "Bingo." He also boasted a high-arcing rainbow jump shot that gave Cleveland's early clubs a much-needed offensive weapon. And later in his career, it was Smith's wild hair that earned him a good share of attention. During a game of H-O-R-S-E at halftime in the 1970s, Bingo refused to attempt an off-the-head shot made by Kevin Grevey because he did not want to mess up his afro.

His longevity also helped Smith become a fan favorite. The Tulsa product played his rookie season with San Diego before coming to Cleveland in the 1970 expansion draft. Ten of the eleven men chosen by the Cavs that day either never played for the team or were gone after four seasons. The exception was Smith, who spent ten years and more than seven hundred games helping the franchise overcome its growing pains.

Bingo led the 1974–75 team in scoring at 15.9 points per game. The following season, he was an integral part of the "Miracle of Richfield." His winning shot in the final seconds of Game 2 helped Cleveland beat Washington for its first-ever playoff series win. Even now, almost thirty years after the Cavaliers retired his jersey (No. 7), Smith remains among the club's top ten in several statistical categories.

Austin Carr

Before there was LeBron James, there was Austin Carr (A. C.). Like James in 2003, Carr was a

No. 1 overall draft choice in 1971. And like James in his first two years, Carr made an instant impact. His 21.2 points per game helped him become the first Cleveland player to make the NBA All-Rookie Team. A. C. kept his scoring average above 20 in each of the next two seasons as well. In 1973–74, he made the NBA All-Star Game.

Carr was a household name by the time he reached the NBA. His high-scoring career at Notre Dame assured wide renown. His name is still splashed all over the NCAA tournament record book. Carr's 61 points, 25 field goals, and 44 field goal attempts remain single-game tourney

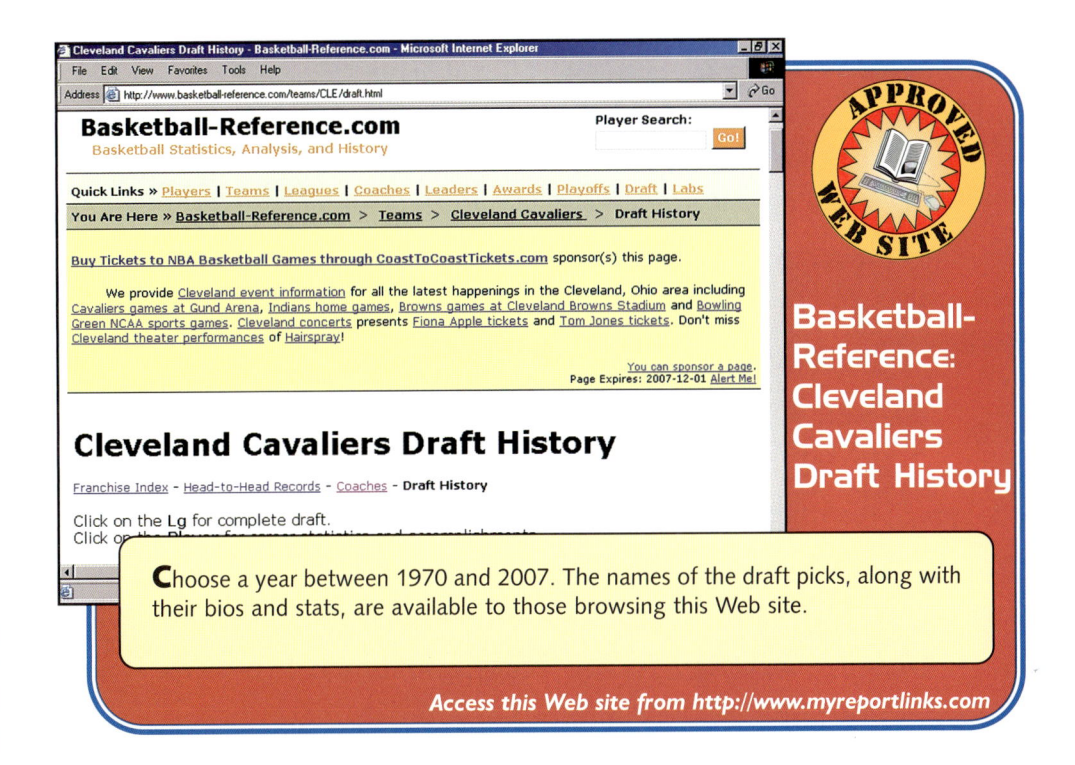

Basketball-Reference: Cleveland Cavaliers Draft History

Choose a year between 1970 and 2007. The names of the draft picks, along with their bios and stats, are available to those browsing this Web site.

Access this Web site from http://www.myreportlinks.com

records. So, too, is his 41.3-point scoring average for his NCAA tournament career. In fact, the next best NCAA Tournament scoring average—posted by Bill Bradley—stands more than seven points behind.

A knee injury requiring surgery in 1974 robbed Carr of some of his explosiveness. However, he remained a Cavs standout for a decade and led the team to three playoff berths. In 1980, Carr won the NBA's J. Walter Kennedy Citizenship Award for his contributions to the Cleveland community. He remains an integral part of the team as a Cavs executive and television analyst.

World B. Free

A friend in Brooklyn gave Lloyd Free the nickname "World" for the 360-degree dunks he fashioned on the playground. The name stuck—so much so, that Free later adopted it legally. His new name was unforgettable, and his flamboyant game was a perfect match.

World never met a shot he did not like. At age forty-six, the community-minded Free was teaching Philadelphia-area youngsters passing techniques during a camp. An onlooker quipped that Free could "count the number of assists he had on one hand."[1] It was an exaggeration for the sake of a laugh, but scoring—not passing—was certainly Free's claim to fame.

The Heroes

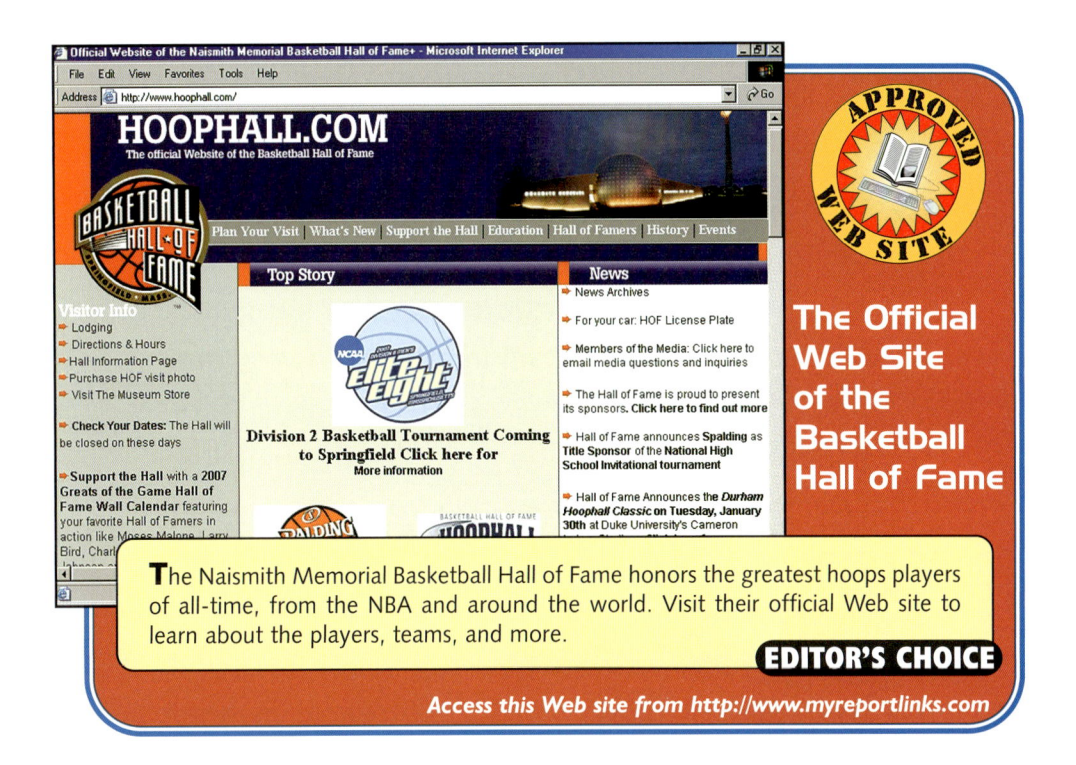

HOOPHALL.COM
The official Website of the Basketball Hall of Fame

The Naismith Memorial Basketball Hall of Fame honors the greatest hoops players of all-time, from the NBA and around the world. Visit their official Web site to learn about the players, teams, and more.

EDITOR'S CHOICE

Access this Web site from http://www.myreportlinks.com

Free averaged more than 20 points per game over a thirteen-year career with the 76ers, Clippers, Warriors, Cavaliers, and Rockets. Free joined the Cavs early in the 1982–83 season and averaged between 22 and 24 points per game in each of the next three years. Said Harry Weltman, the general manager who brought Free to Cleveland, "World made people care about us."[2]

▶ Mike Mitchell

High-scoring forward Mike Mitchell spent most of his career with San Antonio, playing with the likes of George Gervin and Artis Gilmore. However, he opened his career with Cleveland. It was with the

Cavs in 1981 that Mitchell made his only trip to the NBA All-Star Game.

The site for the game was Cleveland's Richfield Coliseum. Mitchell was added to the Eastern Conference roster when Atlanta's Dan Roundfield was forced to withdraw because of an injury. Mitchell was a terrific fill-in. The third-year man from Auburn University totaled 14 points, 4 rebounds, and 2 assists in just fifteen minutes to help the East to a 123–120 victory. A crowd of 20,239 cheered their local favorite wildly. "It was a shock, just walking out there," said Mitchell, who averaged a career-high 24.5 points per game that season. "I never saw 20,000 people cheering for me before. It was very special to me."[3]

The following season, the Cavs traded Mitchell and teammate Roger Phegley to the Spurs for Ron Brewer and Reggie Johnson. Mitchell played six-and-a-half seasons in San Antonio and scored more than 15,000 career points. His all-star memories, however, are 100 percent Cleveland. His Cavs record of four straight games with 30 or more points, set in March 1981, stood for almost a quarter century before LeBron James eclipsed it in December 2005.

Larry Nance

Larry Nance grew up in NASCAR country. It makes sense, then, that the South Carolina native has

The Heroes

Cavaliers News: Top 10 Moments in Cavaliers History

At a Cavaliers game on April 14, 2005, the team announced what the fans voted as the Top 10 Moments in Cavaliers History. Read the list on this Web page.

Access this Web site from http://www.myreportlinks.com

long held an affinity for race cars. Two years after playing in his last NBA game, Nance entered—and won—his first professional drag racing event. It springboarded the three-time NBA All-Star into an NHRA (National Hot Rod Association) driving career that would have to be sensational to match his work on the hardwood.

Nance was an established scorer, tenacious rebounder, and sensational shot-blocker when the Cavs acquired him in a trade with Phoenix in 1988–89. He had won the NBA's inaugural Slam Dunk Contest in 1984. His six-plus years of experience and commitment to defense were precisely what the Cavaliers needed.

With Nance, the Cavs took off. Cleveland reached the playoffs in five of his six years on the club, advancing all the way to the Eastern Conference Finals in 1992. Nance was the first Cavalier in history to make the NBA All-Defensive First Team. With more than two thousand blocked shots, he remains the NBA's career leader among forwards.

Brad Daugherty

His was a short NBA career—eight seasons, all with Cleveland. But Brad Daugherty made the most of it. When he retired due to chronic back problems, he was the Cavaliers' all-time leader in points (10,389), rebounds (5,227), free throws made (2,741) and attempted (3,670), triple doubles (4), and All-Star Game appearances (5).

Daugherty was the man in the middle during Cleveland's most successful run. The team's first No. 1 overall draft choice since Austin Carr in 1971, he arrived along with Mark Price and Ron Harper in 1986. Daugherty, who had won a national championship with the University of North Carolina, needed little time to adjust. He averaged 15.7 points and 8.1 rebounds a game as a rookie. He went on to become one of the NBA's premier centers and a regular 20-point, 10-rebound man.

▲ Cleveland center Brad Daugherty attempts to poke the ball away from Celtics Hall of Famer Larry Bird. Daugherty retired as the leading scorer in Cavaliers history.

Daugherty set a club record, broken by LeBron James in 2006, by scoring 40 points in a 1992 playoff game. That year, his postseason averages of 21.5 points, 10.2 rebounds, and 3.4 assists led Cleveland to the conference finals for only the second time. It was one of five times the team reached the postseason during his eight-year tenure. To this day, Daugherty is considered the best center in Cavaliers history.

Hot Rod Williams

John Williams was dubbed "Hot Rod" as a baby for the way he used to scoot backward on the floor while making "engine sounds." His NBA career also started out in reverse, as he and four of his Tulane University teammates were implicated in a point-shaving scandal. Although charges were eventually dropped, the ordeal cost Williams the 1985–86 season. The NBA would not approve his contract until the case was resolved.

As a Cleveland rookie in 1986–87, Williams scored in double digits for the first of nine successive seasons with the Cavs. That year, he joined Daugherty and Ron Harper on the NBA All-Rookie Team. Williams was a key member of six Cavaliers playoff squads. He filled in at center for an injured Daugherty for more than a full season in the mid-1990s. And by the time he left for Phoenix before the 1995–96 campaign, he had rejected more shots in a Cleveland uniform than any player in history.

Mark Price

Few things have been certain in the roller-coaster history of the Cleveland Cavaliers. One of the exceptions: a Mark Price free throw.

Some said the former Georgia Tech star was too small and too slow for the NBA. But Price helped turn Cleveland into a contender and set an NBA career record for free-throw accuracy (90.4 percent). By the time he retired, coaches at all levels were showing videotapes of Price's flawless shooting technique.

"My dad was a coach, and that was one of his pet peeves," Price explained. "He couldn't stand guys not making free throws. And I didn't want my dad to yell at me."[4] However, turning free throws into automatic points was not Price's only talent. He twice won the NBA's Long Distance Shootout, and he finished in the top ten in assists five times. He played in four NBA All-Star Games, and he was the first Cavs player ever named to the All-NBA First Team (1992–93).

Price's value to the Cavaliers was unmistakable. The 1990–91 campaign, when a torn ACL (anterior cruciate ligament) limited him to sixteen games, was the only season in Price's tenure as starting point guard in which the Cavs failed to reach the playoffs.

Retired Cavaliers guard Mark Price holds up a piece of the old Richfield Coliseum floor. The team retired his uniform number that night, November 13, 1999.

Shawn Kemp

An Indiana high school phenom, Shawn Kemp became a dominant player during an eight-year run in Seattle. The explosive power forward led the Sonics, in separate years, to the NBA's best record and an NBA Finals berth. He also won an Olympic gold medal as a member of "Dream Team II."

In 1997, Seattle traded Kemp to Cleveland in a blockbuster deal involving Vin Baker, Terrell Brandon, and Tyrone Hill. In 1997–98, Kemp tied a Gund Arena record with 20 rebounds in a game and became the first All-Star Game starter in club history. He totaled 12 points, 11 boards, and 4 steals in the contest.

The following season, Kemp set a career high in scoring with 20.5 points per game. Before the 1999–2000 season, his third and final one with the Cavaliers, Kemp was named to the franchise's all-time starting five. He was traded to Portland the following year, and he later scored his 15,000th career point for Orlando.

Zydrunas Ilgauskas

International basketball took off in the 1990s, and the Cavaliers were among the teams that recognized the surge early. In 1996, they spent their first-round pick on Zydrunas Ilgauskas of Lithuania. At seven foot three inches and upwards of 250 pounds, Ilgauskas had averaged 20-plus

▲ This 1998 photo shows Cleveland center Zydrunas Ilgauskas dunking in a game against the Hornets.

The Heroes

points and nearly 13 rebounds per game the previous season. And although a broken bone in his foot caused him to miss the entire 1996–97 campaign, and another foot injury cost him the entire 1999–2000 campaign, he has been a key cog in the Cavaliers' recent climb to contender status.

Ilgauskas made the NBA All-Rookie Team in 1997–98 and was named MVP of the Schick Rookie Game. His next full season was 2002–03, when the Cavs were encouraged to find that his litany of injuries had not robbed him of his effectiveness. Able to score in the post or facing the basket, the big man averaged 17.2 points per

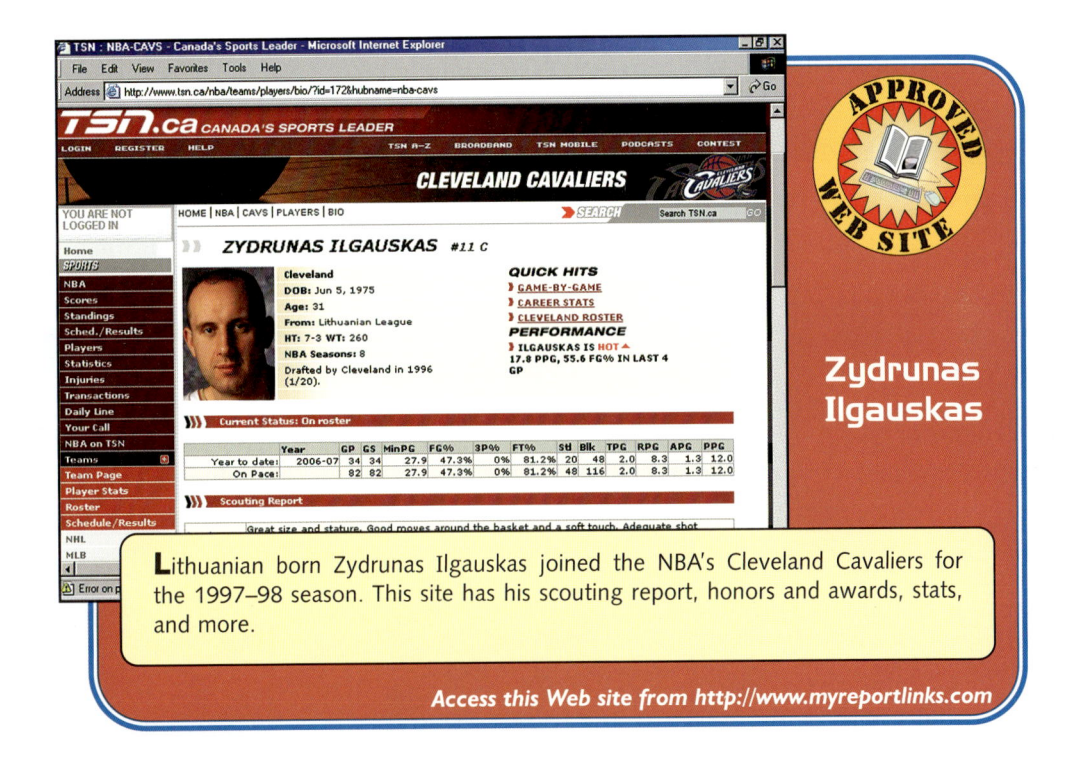

Zydrunas Ilgauskas

Lithuanian born Zydrunas Ilgauskas joined the NBA's Cleveland Cavaliers for the 1997–98 season. This site has his scouting report, honors and awards, stats, and more.

Access this Web site from http://www.myreportlinks.com

Edging toward the basket, LeBron James backs in against Richard Hamilton of the Pistons.

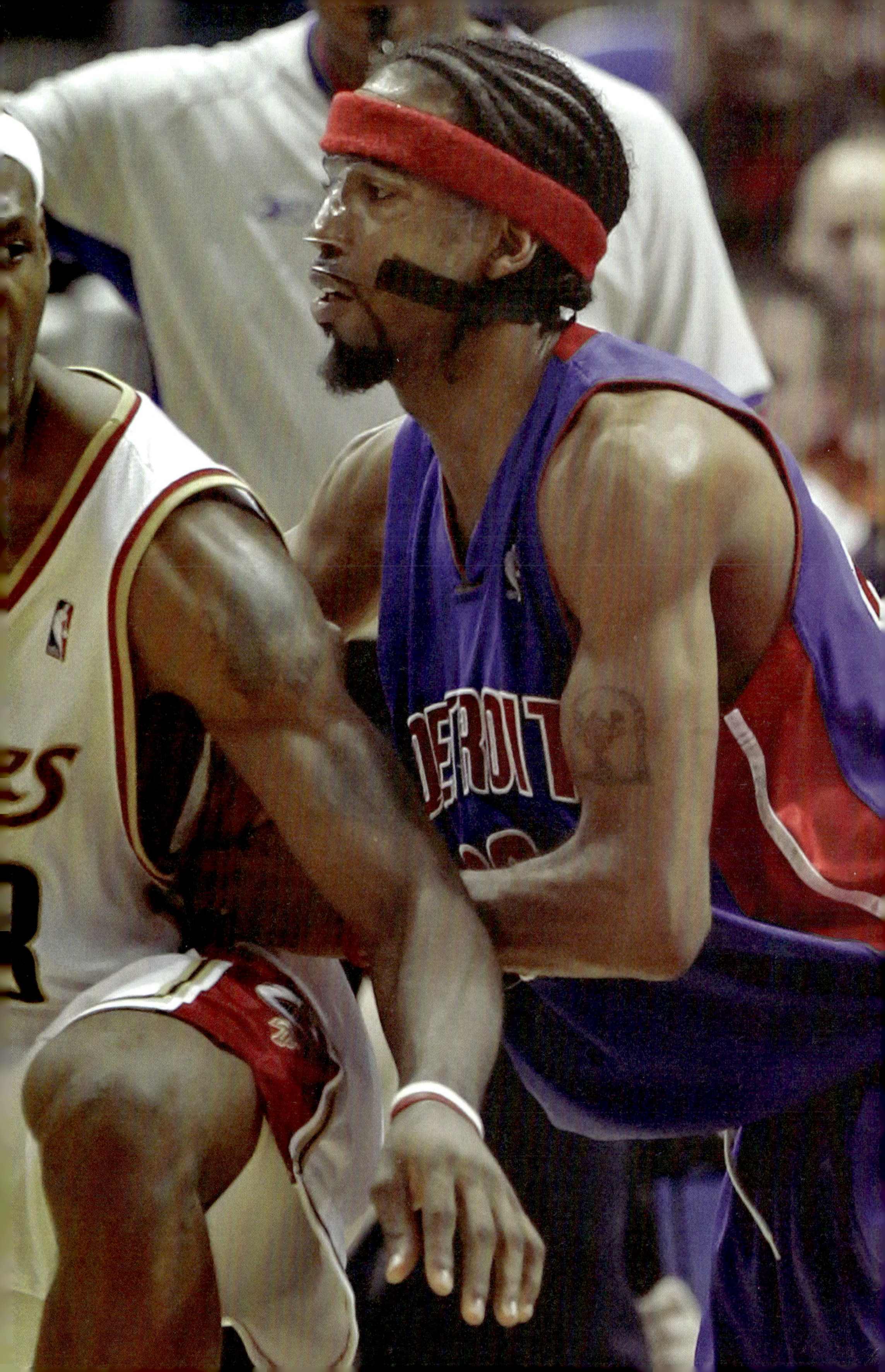
DETROIT

game for a team that slumped to a pre-LeBron 17–65 embarrassment.

The bright side of those dismal days was the arrival of LeBron James with the first pick in the 2003 NBA Draft. With an elite perimeter presence setting up his inside game, Ilgauskas saw his shooting percentage, rebounding average, and overall effectiveness soar. In 2004–05, Ilgauskas played in his second NBA All-Star Game.

LeBron James

He wears No. 23, the same number worn by Michael Jordan. Since he entered the NBA directly from high school in 2003, James has shown that he could join Jordan as a basketball immortal. While watching him dazzle crowds in the 2006 NBA Playoffs, Scottie Pippen said of James, "He's growing into the greatest ever to play the game."[5] Recall that Pippen teamed with Jordan to win six NBA championships with the Chicago Bulls.

Until he wins multiple MVP awards and leads the Cavaliers to championship status, all such comparisons are premature. In the meantime, James wows the world with his explosive scoring, gravity-defying dunks, superior ball skills, and leadership ability. He has given the NBA a marquee attraction like no player since . . . well . . . that other No. 23.

James nearly won an MVP award just three seasons into his career. After ranking third in the NBA in scoring (31.4 PPG) in 2005–06, he finished a close second to the Phoenix Suns' Steve Nash in the MVP balloting. He also became the youngest player ever (21 years, 138 days) to be named to the All-NBA First Team. James's numbers were down only slightly during the 2006–07 season. However, he led the Cavs to the NBA Finals and, in March, became the youngest-ever NBA player to reach 8,000 points.

Will NBA championships follow, as many predict? Time will tell. But it is safe to say that the kid from Akron—No. 23 in your program—is No. 1 in Cleveland's heart.

Report Links

The Internet sites described below can be accessed at http://www.myreportlinks.com

▶ **The Official Site of the Cleveland Cavaliers**
Editor's Choice Visit this official site for the most up-to-date team news.

▶ **The Official Site of LeBron James**
Editor's Choice Find out more about LeBron James from his Web site.

▶ **Cleveland Cavaliers History**
Editor's Choice This site provides a nice overview of Cavaliers history.

▶ **NBA.com**
Editor's Choice The official Web site of the National Basketball Association.

▶ **The Official Web Site of the Basketball Hall of Fame**
Editor's Choice The best players are enshrined in the Naismith Memorial Basketball Hall of Fame.

▶ **Cleveland Cavaliers (1970–Present)**
Editor's Choice An historical overview of the Cleveland Cavaliers.

▶ ***Akron Beacon Journal:* "Cavaliers Replace Veteran Announcer"**
This newspaper article provides the details of Michael Reghi's dismissal.

▶ **Basketball-Reference: Cleveland Cavaliers Coaches**
Information on each Cleveland Cavaliers head coach.

▶ **Basketball-Reference: Cleveland Cavaliers Draft History**
See who the Cavaliers have drafted.

▶ **Cavaliers History: Cleveland Cavaliers Season Summaries**
Season-by-season highlights for the Cleveland Cavaliers.

▶ **Cavaliers History: The Making of a Miracle**
This article chronicles the epic seven-game series that took place in April 1976.

▶ **Cavaliers News: Top 10 Moments in Cavaliers History**
Fans chose the top moments in Cavaliers history.

▶ **Cleveland Arena**
This site has the history and photographs of the Cleveland Arena.

▶ **Cleveland Cavaliers' Jerseys**
Photos and descriptions of each Cleveland jersey.

▶ **Cleveland.com: Cleveland Cavaliers**
Follow the Cavs by reading articles at this online sports section.

Visit "My Toolkit" at www.myreportlinks.com for tips on using the Internet.

MyReportLinks.com Books

Tools   Search   Notes   Discuss   Go!

Report Links

The Internet sites described below can be accessed at http://www.myreportlinks.com

▶ **ESPN.com: The Playoffs**
Visit this ESPN site for a look back at the 2007 NBA Finals.

▶ **Hall of Famers: Leonard "Lenny" Wilkens**
This is a time line of Lenny Wilkens's career.

▶ **Joe Tait: Wham! The Voice of the Cavaliers**
Read a bio of Cavaliers announcer Joe Tait.

▶ **LeBron James**
Read about LeBron James when you visit this site.

▶ **Most Valuable Network: Cavalier Attitude**
This popular blog is exclusively about the Cleveland Cavaliers.

▶ **NBA's Greatest Moments: Jordan Hits "The Shot"**
This online article depicts perhaps the toughest moment in Cavs history.

▶ **Nick J. Mileti: Cleveland's Illustrious Italian**
Nick Mileti was the original owner of the Cleveland Cavaliers.

▶ **Quicken Loans Arena**
This site offers a good description of the Quicken Loans Arena.

▶ **The Sporting News: "No Laughing at Cavaliers Any More"**
This *Sporting News* article from 1976 looks at the Cavaliers' breakout season.

▶ **The Sun News: "No Ordinary Voice in the Crowd"**
An interview with renowned play-by-play man Joe Tait.

▶ **The Trust for Public Land: The Rise and Fall of Richfield Coliseum**
A short history of the Richfield Coliseum.

▶ **USA Basketball: LeBron James**
This USA Basketball.com site has a time line of LeBron James's career.

▶ **Washington Post: "Ferry Rises From Front Row to the Cavaliers' Front Office"**
Find out more about how Danny Ferry was picked to run the team.

▶ **Washington Post: "Loyalty Lands Brown in Greener Pastures"**
An article summarizing Mike Brown's rise to head coach of the Cavs.

▶ **Zydrunas Ilgauskas**
This player page for Ilgauskas contains his career stats.

Any comments? Contact us: comments@myreportlinks.com

CAREER

HEAD COACH	SEASONS	W	L	PCT.	Playoffs W	L
Bill Fitch	1970-71 to 1978-79	304	434	.412	7	11
Stan Albeck	1979-80	37	45	.451	—	—
Bill Musselman	1980-81, 1981-82	27	67	.287	—	—
Don Delaney	1980-81 to 1981-82	7	21	.250	—	—
Bob Kloppenburg	1981-82	0	1	.000	—	—
Chuck Daly	1981-82	9	32	.220	—	—
Tom Nissalke	1982-83 to 1983-84	51	113	.311	—	—
George Karl	1984-85 to 1985-86	61	88	.409	1	3
Gene Littles	1985-86	4	11	.267	—	—
Lenny Wilkens	1986-87 to 1992-93	316	258	.551	18	23
Mike Fratello	1993-94 to 1998-99	248	230	.519	2	12
Randy Wittman	1999-00 to 2000-01	62	102	.378	—	—
John Lucas	2001-02 to 2002-03	37	87	.298	—	—
Keith Smart	2002-03	9	31	.225	—	—
Paul Silas	2003-04 to 2004-05	69	77	.473	—	—
Brendan Malone	2004-05	8	10	.444	—	—
Mike Brown	2005-07	100	64	.610	19	13

SEASONS=Seasons coaching Cavs   W=Wins   L=Losses   PCT.=Winning Percentage

STATS

PLAYER	SEASONS	YRS	G	REB	AST	BLK	STL	PTS	PPG
Butch Beard	1971-72 1975-76	9	605	2,042	2,189	36	499	5,622	9.3
Austin Carr	1971-80	10	682	1,990	1,878	66	433	10,473	15.4
Brad Daugherty	1986-94	8	548	5,227	2,028	397	422	10,389	19.0
World B. Free	1983-86	13	866	2,430	3,319	223	910	17,955	20.3
Drew Gooden	2004-07	5	390	3,070	446	260	314	4,703	12.1
Larry Hughes	2005-07	9	550	2,503	1,846	209	867	8,352	15.2
Zydrunas Ilgauskas	1997-2007	9	569	4,387	713	1,015	322	8,275	14.5
LeBron James	2003-07	4	316	2,102	2,033	231	555	8,439	26.7
John Johnson	1970-73	12	869	4,778	3,285	235	487	11,200	12.9
Shawn Kemp	1997-2000	14	1,051	8,834	1,704	1,279	1,185	15,347	14.6
Mike Mitchell	1978-82	10	759	4,246	1,010	400	530	15,016	19.8
Larry Nance	1988-94	13	920	7,352	2,393	2,027	872	15,687	17.1
Mark Price	1986-95	12	722	1,848	4,863	76	860	10,989	15.2
Bobby "Bingo" Smith	1970-80	11	865	3,630	1,734	167	431	10,882	12.6
Walt Wesley	1970-73	10	590	3,243	385	25	16	5,002	8.5
John "Hot Rod" Williams	1986–95	13	887	5,998	1,591	1,456	747	9,784	11.0

SEASONS=Seasons with Cavs YRS=Years in the NBA G=Games played REB=Rebounds
AST=Assists BLK=Blocks STL=Steals PTS=Points
PPG=Points per game

Glossary

assist—The last pass made to a teammate who is then able to make a basket.

caliber—A level of excellence or importance.

double figures—Two-digit numbers, specifically any number between 10 and 99.

draft—The selection of college and foreign players each year by NBA teams. Normally the teams with the worst records have the best chance of choosing first.

forward—The two players on a basketball team who stand on either side of the center. Forwards are usually among the taller players counted on for inside scoring and rebounding.

franchise—A team that has membership in a professional sports league.

free agent—A professional player who is free to negotiate a contract with any team.

free throw—A shot awarded a player who is fouled by an opponent. Each free throw is taken from the foul line and counts for one point.

general manager—The person in charge of building the team by getting players either through the draft or by trades. The general manager is in charge of team matters not handled by the coaching staff.

inbound pass—When one player throws the ball to a teammate from the sidelines of the court.

ledger—Record.

offense—The team who has possession of the ball.

pick—A play in basketball where one offensive player will step in front of a defender who is trying to defend another offensive player. This will free up the offensive player to cut to the basket unguarded.

point guard—The player on a basketball team who generally handles the ball best. The job of the point guard is to bring the ball up the court and run the offense.

point-shaving scandal—When players of the team favored to win purposely play poorly so that the final score will be much closer than it should be. This way, people betting on the team to cover the point spread will lose. Point shaving is illegal.

rebound—The retrieving of a ball after a missed shot.

romp—An easy win.

rookie—Name given to a first-year player in a major professional sport.

swingman—A player capable of playing more that one position on the basketball court, usually a player who can play guard or forward.

tenure—Time spent with an organization or in a job.

tourney—Tournament.

trailblazer—Pioneer or leader.

triple-double—When a player tallies ten or more of three of the following categories in one game: points, rebounds, assists, blocked shots, and steals.

Chapter Notes

Chapter 1. Home, James

1. "Something to Cheer," *SI.com,* May 22, 2003, <http://sportsillustrated.cnn.com/basketball/nba/2003/draft/news/2003/05/22/cavs_fans_ap/> (November 29, 2006).

2. Ibid.

3. Tom Canavan, "Cavaliers win LeBron Lottery," *USA Today*, May 22, 2003, <http://www.usatoday.com/sports/basketball/draft/2003-05-22-lottery-order_x.htm> (November 29, 2006).

4. Ibid.

5. Ibid.

Chapter 2. Fitch's Franchise

1. "Cavaliers Unofficial All-Time Teams," *NBA.com,* n.d., <http://www.nba.com/cavaliers/news/all_time_teams_050726.html> (November 29, 2006).

2. Bill Nichols, "Cavaliers Lose in NBA Debut," *The Cleveland Plain Dealer,* October 15, 1970, <http://www.lkwdpl.org/nworth/nbadebut.htm> (November 29, 2006).

3. Bill Nichols, "No Laughing at Cavaliers Any More," *The Sporting News,* March 20, 1976, <http://www.lkwdpl.org/lfiles/nichols/cavs1976.htm> (November 29, 2006).

4. Ibid.

Chapter 3. Title Contender

1. "The Top 35 Moments in Cavaliers History," *NBA.com,* n.d., <http://www.nba.com/cavaliers/news/top_35_test3.html> (November 29, 2006).

2. "Sports People; Wilkens to Cavaliers," *The New York Times,* July 10, 1986, <http://query.nytimes.com/gst/fullpage.html?res=9A0DE5DC153BF933A25754C0A960948260> (November 29, 2006).

3. Rick Weinberg, "81: With 'The Shot,' Jordan eliminates Cavs at buzzer," *ESPN.com,* n.d., <http://sports.espn.go.com/espn/espn25/story?page=moments/81> (November 29, 2006).

4. Danny O'Neil, "A Moment with . . . Craig Ehlo, former WSU and NBA player," *Seattle Post-Intelligencer,* March 26, 2003, <http://seattlepi.nwsource.com/basketball/114239_ehlo26.shtml> (November 29, 2006).

5. "Chat with Cavaliers Radio Play-by-Play Announcer Joe Tait," *NBA.com,* n.d., <http://proxy.espn.go.com/chat/chatNBA?event_id=11149> (November 29, 2006).

Chapter 4. The King James Era

1. "He's the real deal," *ESPN.com,* October 30, 2003, <http://sports.espn.go.com/espn/print?id=1650462&type=story> (November 29, 2006).

2. Ibid.

3. "LeBron is youngest to get triple-double," *CHINAdaily,* January 20, 2005, <http://www.chinadaily.com.cn/english/doc/2005-01/20/content_410860.htm> (November 29, 2006).

4. Ibid.

5. "Cavaliers Name Mike Brown Head Coach," *NBA.com,* June 2, 2005, <http://www.nba.com/cavaliers/news/brown_coach_050602.html> (November 29, 2006).

6. "Cavs Officially Hire Mike Brown," *USA Today,* June 1, 2005, <http://www.usatoday.com/sports/basketball/nba/cavaliers/2005-06-01-mike-brown-hiring_x.htm> (November 29, 2006).

7. Chris Bubeck, "One-on-One," *NBA.com,* n.d., <http://www.nba.com/aroundtheassociation/regular_season_review_3.html> (November 29, 2006).

8. Sports Network, "James' triple-double gives Cleveland a 1–0 series lead," *sacbee.com,* April 22, 2006, <http://www.sacbee.com/24hour/sports/basketball/nba/story/3268293p-12063241c.html> (May 17, 2006).

Chapter 5. Cavs in Charge

1. "Scouting; Bad to Worse," *The New York Times,* December 31, 1985, <http://query.nytimes.com/gst/fullpage.html?res=9503E0DF103BF932A05751C1A963948260&n=Top%2fNews%2fSports%2fPro%20Basketball%2fNational%20Basketball%20Association%2fCleveland%20Cavaliers> (November 29, 2006).

2. Bill Nichols, "No Laughing at Cavaliers Any More," *The Sporting News,* March 20, 1976, <http://www.lkwdpl.org/lfiles/nichols/cavs1976.htm> (November 29, 2006).

3. Ibid.

4. "The Inside Game," *The University of Akron Press,* n.d., <http://www3.uakron.edu/uapress/embry.html> (November 29, 2006).

5. NBA Encyclopedia: Playoff Edition, "Lenny Wilkens Bio," *NBA.com,* n.d., <http://www.nba.com/history/players/wilkens_bio.html> (November 29, 2006).

6. Joe Menzer, "Playing With Fire," *The Sporting*

News, January 17, 1994, <http://www.highbeam.com/library/docfree.asp?DOCID=1G1:14957703&ctrlInfo=Round19%3AMode19a%3ADocG%3AResult&ao=> (November 29, 2006).

7. Ibid.

8. Scots Scoop, "Tait Broadcasts 2,500th Game," *Monmouth College,* December 11, 2002, <http://www.monm.edu/SportsInfo/scots-scoop/2002/12-11-02.htm> (November 29, 2006).

9. Michael Lee, "Ferry Rises From Front Row To the Cavaliers' Front Office," *The Washington Post,* November 15, 2005, <http://www.washingtonpost.com/wpdyn/content/article/2005/11/14/AR2005111401520.html> (May 25, 2006).

Chapter 6. Game Day

1. Michael K. McIntyre, "Lovin' Life in 'Loudville,'" *The Cleveland Plain Dealer,* May 16, 2006, <http://www.cleveland.com/nba/plaindealer/index.ssf?/base/sports/114778264664380.xml&coll=2> (November 29, 2006).

2. Ibid.

3. "New Cavs.com Unveiled," *NBA.com,* September 14, 2005, <http://www.nba.com/cavaliers/news/cavsdotcom_unveiled_050914.html> (November 29, 2006).

Chapter 7. The Heroes

1. "Making a World of a Difference," *Northeast Times,* July 26, 2000, <http://www.northeasttimes.com/2000/0726/worldofdifference.html> (November 29, 2006).

2. Terry Pluto, "Free meant world to Cavs. Retire No. 21," *Akron Beacon-Journal,* November 29, 2005, <http://www.ohio.com/mld/ohio/sports/13281738.htm> (June 10, 2006).

3. Bill Nichols, "All-Star Memories," *Tip-Off,* n.d., <http://www.lkwdpl.org/lfiles/nichols/cavs.htm> (November 29, 2006).

4. Richard Deitsch, "Q&A: Mark Price," *CNNSI.com,* March 24, 2006, <http://sportsillustrated.cnn.com/2006/writers/richard_deitsch/03/24/price_qa/1.html> (November 29, 2006).

5. Sam Smith, "LJ better than MJ? On the way, at least," *Chicago Tribune,* May 19, 2006, <http://www.chicagotribune.com/sports/columnists/cs0605190176may19,1,6261555.column?coll=chi-sportscolumnist-hed> (June 15, 2006).

Further Reading

Gordon, Roger. *Tales From the Cleveland Cavaliers: The Rookie Season of LeBron James.* Champaign, Ill.: Sports Publishing, LLC, 2004.

Grabowski, John J., and Diane Ewart Grabowski. *Cleveland Then & Now.* San Diego, Calif.: Thunder Bay Press, 2002.

Hareas, John. *NBA's Greatest.* New York: DK Publishing, 2003.

Hareas, John. *NBA Slam.* New York: Scholastic, 2000.

Herzog, Brad. *Hoopmania: The Book of Basketball History and Trivia.* New York: Rosen Pub. Group, 2003.

LeBoutillier, Nate. *The Story of the Cleveland Cavaliers.* Mankato, Minn.: Creative Education, 2006.

Morgan, David Lee, Jr. *LeBron James: The Rise of a Star.* Cleveland: Gray & Company Publishers, 2003.

Schnakenberg, Robert E. *The Central Division: the Atlanta Hawks, the Chicago Bulls, the Cleveland Cavaliers, the Detroit Pistons, the Indiana Pacers, the Milwaukee Bucks, the New Orleans Hornets, and the Toronto Raptors.* Chanhassen, Minn.: Child's World, 2004.

Smallwood, John N. *Yesterday's Heroes: A Journey Through the History of African-American Superstars in the NBA.* New York: Scholastic, 2001.

Stern, David J. *The Official NBA Basketball Encyclopedia.* New York: Doubleday, 2000.

Wilkens, Lenny. *Unguarded: My Forty Years Surviving in the NBA.* New York: Simon & Schuster, 2001.

Index

A
Albeck, Stan, 29–30
American Basketball League (ABL), 16, 18
Anderson, Derek, 46
attendance records, 53–54

B
Barnett, Dick, 16
Baumholtz, Frankie, 15–16
Beard, Alfred (Butch), 25
Beefcake on the Lake, 92
Bing, Dave, *14*
Boozer, Carlos, 53
Boston Celtics, 5, 42–43
Boston Red Sox, 7
Brandon, Terrell, 45
Brown, Mike
    as head coach, 5, 55, 58, 59
    photograph of, *60*

C
Carlisle, Rick, 55
Carr, Austin
    as 30th anniversary team member, 5, 49
    1978–79 season, 29
    acquisition of, 5, 23–24
    described, 96–98
    photograph of, *22*
Cavalier Girls, 91
Cavaliers Web site, 92–93
Central Division titles
    1976, 5, *14*, 26–28, 71–74
    1992, 41
    2005–06, 59
Chenier, Phil, 27
Chicago Bulls, 5, 39–41, 43
Chones, Jim, 26, 29
Cincinnati Royals, 23
Cleamons, Jim, *14*, 27
Clemens, Barry, 25
Cleveland Arena, 19, 20, 23
Cleveland Browns, 8
Cleveland Indians, 7
Cleveland Pipers, 16–18
Cleveland Rebels, 15–16
Cox, Johnny, 16

D
Daly, Chuck, 30
Daugherty, Brad
    as 30th anniversary team member, 5, 49
    acquisition of, 34
    All-Star honors, 5, 34, 38
    described, 102–104
    retirement of, 45
Davis, Johnny, 35
Delaney, Don, 30
Denver Nuggets, 9
Detroit Pistons, 66, 67

E
Eastern Conference Finals
    1976, 28
    1992, 5, 32, 42–43
Eastern Conference quarterfinals, 2006, 65
Eastern Conference semifinals
    1992–93, 43
    2006, 65–66, *84*, 85
Ehlo, Craig, 36, 39–41
Ellis, LeRoy, 23
Embry, Wayne
    described, 74–76
    as head coach, 5, 36
    NBA Executive of the Year honors, 47
    photograph of, *73*

F
Ferry, Danny, 58–59, *61*, 81–83
Fitch, Bill
    described, 69–70
    as head coach, 19–21, 23, 25
    as NBA Coach of the Year, 27, 70–71, 74
    photograph of, *68*
    resignation of, 29
Fratello, Mike
    described, 78–81
    as head coach, 5, 43, 46, 47
    photograph of, *77*
Frazier, Walt, 29

Index

Free, World B., *94,* 98–99

G
Gilbert, Dan, 5
Gooden, Drew, *63,* 66
Granik, Russ, 10, *12*
Gund, George, 5, *12,* 30–31
Gund, Gordon, 5, 13, 30–31, 36
Gund Arena, 5, 44, 86. *See also* Quicken Loans Arena.

H
Harper, Ron, 34
Henderson, Cedric, 46
Hill, Tyrone, 45
Hinson, Roy, 33–34
history of team
   1970–71 season, 5, 19–23
   1971–76 seasons, 24–25
   1976–77 season, 28–29
   1977–78 playoffs, 5
   1979–82 seasons, 5, 29–30
   1988–89 season, 5, 38–41
   1989–93 season, 5, 41–43
   1993–95 seasons, 43–45
   1995–97 seasons, 5, 45
   1997–2001 seasons, 46–47, 49
   2002–03 season, 5, 8–9, 49
   2003–04 season, 5, 51–54
   2004–05 season, 5, 54–59
   2005–06 season, 5, 59–65
   2006–07 season, 66–67
   acquisition of, 5, 30–31
Hughes, Larry, 66

I
Ilgauskas, Zydrunas
   2006–07 season, 66
   All-Star honors, 5, 46
   described, 107–112
   Indiana Pacers, 47

J
James, LeBron
   2004–05 season, 54–59
   2005–06 season, 5, 59–62
   2006–07 season, 66–67
   acquisition of, 5, 6, 8–13, 51–52
   described, 112–113
   Eastern Conference quarterfinals, 2006, 65
   history, pre-draft, 10–11, 51
   MVP honors, 62, 65
   photograph of, *50, 56, 110–111*
   Rookie of the Year honors, 5
   rookie record, 67
jerseys, 44, 53–54
Johnson, John, 23
Jordan, Michael, 5, 38–41, 53

K
Karl, George, 31
Kemp, Shawn
   as 30th anniversary team member, 5, 49
   All-Star honors, 5
   described, 107
   photograph of, *48*
King Headspin, 91
Kloppenburg, Bob, 30
Knight, Brevin, 46

L
Lewis, Bobby, 21
Littles, Gene, 31
Los Angeles Lakers, 24, 29–30
Lucas, Jerry, *17,* 18
Lucas, John, 49

M
Malone, Brendan, 54
Marshall, Donyell, 62
McClendon, John, 16
McLeod, Frank, 92
Miami Heat, 64
Mileti, Nick, 18, 19, 25
Miller, Andre, 5
Miracle of Richfield, 25–28
Mitchell, Mike, 29, 99–100
Moondog, 90–91
Musselman, Bill, 30

N

Nance, Larry
  as 30th anniversary team member, 5, *32,* 49
  in 1988–89 season, 39
  All-Star honors, 5, 38
  described, 100–102
  retirement of, 45

National Basketball Association (NBA)
  attendance records, 54
  Cleveland franchise granted by, 19
  first-round draft pick bonuses granted by, 30
  and the Pipers, 18
  Web site, 89

NBA All-Star Weekend 1997, 45
Newman, Johnny, 36
New Orleans Hornets, 59
New York Knickerbockers, 5, 16, 29
Nissalke, Tom, 30–31
Nixon, Norm, 30

P

Paxson, Jim, 47
Philadelphia 76ers, 5, 33–34
Price, Mark
  as 30th anniversary team member, 5, 49
  acquisition of, 34–36
  All-Star honors, 5, 38, 43
  described, 105–106
  retirement of, 45

Q

Quicken Loans Arena. *See also* Gund Arena.
  amenities, 88
  described, 85–88
  game night activities, 89–90
  photograph of, *84*
  ticket prices, 86

R

Richfield Coliseum, 5, 24, 25
Russell, Michael (Campy), 29

S

Sadowski, Ed, 15
Scream Team, 91–92
Sedra, Olivier, 89–90
Sellers, Brad, 39
Sharman, Bill, 16
Silas, Paul, 54
Smart, Keith, 49
Smith, Bobby (Bingo), 21, 23, 27, 29, 95–96
Snow, Eric, 66
Snyder, Dick, 27
Snyder, Mike, 92
Steinbrenner, George, 16–19
Stepien, Ted, 30

T

Tait, Joe, 41, 42, 81–82, 89, 92
The Shot, 38–40
Thurmond, Nate, 26

U

Unseld, Wes, 27, 81

W

Wade, Dwyane, 64
Warren, John, 23
Washington Bullets, 5, 27, 29
Wesley, Walt, 23
Wilkens, Lenny
  acquisition of, 25
  assists per game honors, 5, 25
  described, 75–78
  as Eastern Conference All-Star Team coach, 38
  as head coach, 5, 36
  NBA All-Star honors, 45
  photograph of, *37*
  resignation of, 43, 79
Williams, John (Hot Rod), 104–105
Wittman, Randy, 47, 49